P9-DBP-338

NO 07 '01	DATE DUE	
NO 20 '01	DE 16 '04	
DE 04 '01	AP 19 '05	
JA 24 '02	OC 26 '05	
MR 07 '02		
AP 05 '02	OCT 1 4 '08	
AP 26 '02	OCT 2 0 '08	
MY 07 '03	JN 0 5 10	
DE 02 '03		
FE 23 '04		
OC 21 '04		
NO 08 '04		

Desdemona-Twelve Going on
Desperate
Beverly Keller
AR B.L.: 5.0
Points: 5.0

DESDEMONA-
Twelve Going on Desperate

by Beverly Keller

HarperTrophy®
A Division of HarperCollins*Publishers*

Desdemona—Twelve Going on Desperate
Copyright © 1986 by Beverly Keller
Published by arrangement with William Morrow & Co., Inc.
All rights reserved. No part of this book may be used or
reproduced in any manner whatsoever without written
permission except in the case of brief quotations embodied in
critical articles and reviews. Printed in the United States of
America. For information address HarperCollins Children's
Books, a division of HarperCollins Publishers,
10 East 53rd Street, New York, NY 10022.

Library of Congress Cataloging-in-Publication Data
Keller, Beverly.
    Desdemona—twelve going on desperate.

    Summary: Calamity stalks a seventh grader in the form of
social disasters, and throughout it all, to her great embarrass-
ment, she keeps running into the most attractive boy in school.
    [1. Single-parent family—Fiction.   2. Schools—Fiction
3. Humorous stories.]   I. Title.
PZ7.K2813De   1986   87-45287
ISBN 0-06-440226-6

Published in hardcover by Lothrop, Lee & Shepard Books.
First Harper Trophy edition, 1988.

To Dulce

one

Bramwell Grove started destroying my life before I ever met him.

It began with a morning telephone call in early November. My father left the twins and me at the breakfast table while he went to answer it.

"That was Harley Grove," he said when he came back. "He wants to bring his brother Bramwell over to see our house."

The twins were too young to be interested, but I was puzzled. "Why would our landlord want to show his brother our house?"

My father looked the way he does when the car's engine makes a new and sinister sound he can barely hear. "I don't know, Dez. Something's going on, though. I put him off until after I get back from the mental health convention, but I want you all to come right home from school today and clean your room. It's going to take a week to make this house fit to see."

Mrs. Farisee, our housekeeper, set a platter of

1

pancakes down so hard the table shivered. She gazed at my father silently. Mrs. Farisee is twenty pounds heavier and at least twenty years older than he, and her stare would make a barbarian tremble.

She had a right to be offended. Mrs. Farisee's attitude toward dirt and dust and clutter is "No quarter!" She kept the ancient stove and linoleum and our battered furniture polished, but she considered anything lurking in the yard or under our beds beyond her jurisdiction.

"I mean general repairs," my father murmured hastily, "all the things I've been meaning to get around to."

When he left for work, he looked worried. He had reason, considering the condition of our house.

Mrs. Farisee was rebuttoning my brother's coat when Sherman Grove came to walk us to school.

Before he had started kindergarten, Antony took his clothes off publicly whenever he felt at odds with things. In a few weeks, the education system had civilized him so that he only buttoned his coat wrong every morning. I couldn't help feeling a little sad that he'd given in so easily.

The school had put Antony in morning session and Aida in afternoon, I suppose on the theory that twins can become over-dependent on each other.

It was true that my brother and sister had never been very interested in other people. Since they understood each other without speaking, they had a full social life without anybody else.

My father was afraid the forced separation might make them more dependent on each other out of school, but he didn't argue with the administration. "They probably buy the myth that a psychologist's kids have more problems than most," he said. "If I try throwing my weight around, they'll start looking for quirks in my kids."

So I walked Antony to school in the morning and walked Aida home in the afternoon.

Sherman, of course, walked with me both ways. Except for sleeping at home, he spent most of his free time with my family.

It hadn't been easy starting junior high only months after we moved to this town. It seemed as if all the other girls in the school had known one another from birth. I didn't understand their jokes, and I was sure I didn't dress right, and I was worried about acting so friendly I'd seem desperate or so cool I'd seem snobbish. While a few girls talked to me, none had ever asked me over or walked home with me or sat with me at lunch.

Being new in junior high is like being the sister of twins, circling people who are in a huddle, getting only a glimpse over their shoulders now and then.

It didn't do me any good socially to be trailed everywhere by my landlord's eleven-year-old son, a loner who was widely regarded as a wimp.

Sherman was also the best friend I'd ever had. When I was sick with the flu, he lugged his VCR all the way to our house, with his favorite tapes. It

3

takes a lot of devotion for an eleven-year-old to let himself be seen in public pulling a red wagon.

I owed Sherman more than that. When his father found out we had three dogs and gave us an eviction notice, it was Sherman who saved us. At the town's big Founder's Day picnic, he managed to get lost. My father and Shirley Miller and I found Sherman, and even had our pictures in the paper with the caption *Rescuers of Grove Boy.* While Harley Grove could hardly evict us after that, he rented to us grudgingly. Knowing Sherman was kind of like having a friend at court. How could I tell him he was a social catastrophe?

We had to wait while Mrs. Farisee made Antony take off his rain boots and put them on the proper feet. Then he and Sherman and I hurried out the door.

It's a comfort to have anybody, *anybody,* to walk with when you're afraid you're late for school.

Even at twelve and a half, with years of on-time attendance behind me, I remembered how it felt to walk to school late and alone. I doubt if anyone ever forgets completely.

Your parents go to bed without setting the alarm, or without changing the clock for daylight saving time, or the broken shoelace you'd tied together breaks again with no room for another knot, or you spill juice down your sweater, or you can't find your books.

The worst, the very worst, is when your parents

4

know you're so late they don't even try to rush you. Grim, deadly calm, they make you sit down and try to eat breakfast.

By the time you dash out the door, you're terrified. Running, you start to have delusions. You imagine that it's not really that late, that in another block you'll see other kids headed for school. But your stomach knows.

You strain for the sight of even one other wretched straggler, but you know you are so late you'd be better off going home. You can imagine walking home, but you can't imagine actually walking in the door. *And what if your parents forced you to walk right back to school, alone, and later than anybody had ever been?*

Just remembering made me walk faster. Sherman and Antony hurried to keep up with me.

Then we saw some kids ahead of us, ambling along and goofing around, and more coming down the side streets.

Now that I knew we weren't late, I slowed down, so we wouldn't catch up with anybody walking to junior high. Being in the company of a kindergartner and a seventh-grader who looked young for his age, the last thing I wanted was to be noticed.

The dozen blocks from our house to the grade school were like an introduction to the town. A block after the street where we lived, the houses were bigger than ours, some with newer paint, but all with single-car garages. A couple of blocks after

5

that, the houses were bigger yet, and some driveways had a car *and* a camper in them. Then we came to the streets where the houses had two-car garages and the people kept their vehicles inside, so there were no oil stains on the driveways.

Along the street to our right, the front yards were wide and deep. I'd walked down there once or twice, all the way to where the yards had curved driveways and gardeners with leaf blowers tidying the lawns.

Mike Harbinger lived in that neighborhood. On my way to school I'd sometimes see him coming down the street with his friends, a gaggle of little kids tagging after them.

I would have planned my mornings around not letting Mike Harbinger see me with Sherman, except that I knew Mike Harbinger would not see me if I wore sparklers between my teeth. At fifteen, Mike was over six feet tall and not even gangly. He had thick blond hair and brown eyes, he'd never worn braces, and nobody knew anybody who'd ever seen him with a pimple. I knew a lot about him just from listening to other girls. If you were anywhere around junior high school girls, you couldn't avoid hearing about him. He'd been on the honor roll ever since grade school. He was the high school's best hope for the next four years in basketball, football, and track.

Even girls who looked old enough to be high school sophomores hung around the football field after school watching him at practice.

A few times, when Sherman had a cold or stayed after school to work on a project, I walked Aida home by way of the football field. She didn't even complain until we dawdled down to barely moving.

If Mike was aware of all the attention he attracted, he never acted like it. Maybe he'd been admired so long he'd just stopped noticing. He might not have realized how many girls were watching him, since two or three of the guys he hung out with were almost as gorgeous as he. The rest of his friends ranged from good athletes with average looks to a couple of guys who couldn't make it to school without tripping on the curbs.

While Mike Harbinger was clearly out of reach, a few super-popular girls in my school, like Marti Dunnigan and Kerri White, didn't let reality discourage them. Every morning at our lockers they went through the same breathless routine: "Did you see him? Did you see him look at me? Didn't he?" "I know! I know! I think he looked at me, too!"

This morning there was no sign of Mike or his crowd, and I knew I wasn't late for school, so I was able to think of other things. "Your dad called my father this morning," I told Sherman. "He wants to bring your uncle over to see our house. Why, do you suppose?"

"Because he's up to no good, that's why."

Sherman is brilliant, in his own way. He's interested in a great range of things. None of them seemed likely to enhance his social life. His room was full of state-of-the-art electronics and volumes on ecology, archeology, and geology—even his father's outdated real estate manuals and books like *Dress for Success* and *How to Be Your Own Best Friend*.

"When your landlord shows somebody the place you're renting," he went on soberly, "it means he wants to sell it or move in himself. Nobody in my family would live in a dump like yours, and anybody who bought it would either raise the rent or have some kind of deal going. My uncle wouldn't piddle around with buying one crummy house at a time. That means there's something in the works."

Right away, I felt that old rock in my stomach, a mossy boulder sitting in a dank, chill cave. As we crossed the street, I took Antony's hand. "That means I should worry, right?"

"It means that if my Uncle Bramwell buys, you're out." Sherman reached for Antony's other hand. "You could leave the house a mess, but that would be risky. If Bramwell didn't buy it, my father might blame you. He only lets you stay with the dogs because you and your dad—and Shirley Miller—had your picture in the paper the time you found me after I got lost." Sherman always paused a moment after he said "Shirley Miller." Shirley was over thirty, not flashy or beautiful. She had a fine face, though, lean, with clear tanned skin and white even teeth and green eyes with little laugh crinkles at the corners. She was tall and thin, and she moved like a dancer or a runner. The best thing about Shirley was that you knew she acted how she

8

really was: honest and funny and very smart. When we found Sherman, it was Shirley who had scrambled down into the gulley and boosted him up to my father and me.

Poor Sherman, in love with his best friend's father's girl.

"My father couldn't throw you out after that without looking tacky," Sherman went on. "To people like my parents, looking tacky is almost as bad as losing money. So if the place is such a mess my uncle doesn't buy it, my father will be stuck with it, and then he'll be sure to kick you out."

I stopped, not even caring who saw us. "Wait a minute. What about looking tacky?"

"It's been months since you guys rescued me. Did you think he'd be grateful forever?"

As we neared the grade school, Antony watched the kindergarten kids running and talking and laughing. He freed his hands from ours, but he stayed close beside me.

"The other possibility," Sherman said thoughtfully, "is that if the place looks as bad as usual, Bramwell will talk my father into lowering the price, buy it, and kick you out. Tacky would not bother my uncle."

We entered the grade school grounds, Antony so close to me I was in danger of tripping over him. I took him to the door, as I did every morning. "Be sure to come right home," I told him.

He nodded, and trudged through the door by himself.

For a minute, I wondered if Antony and Aida and I were doomed to be social disasters forever. But I had more urgent worries. As Sherman and I headed for our junior high, I asked, "Why would your uncle want a two-bedroom cottage with one bathroom and worn-out linoleum? You said he doesn't fool around with one crummy house at a time."

"Remember when Mr. Troup put his house up for sale and my father tried to buy it? After my father finally agreed to pay the asking price, Mr. Troup decided not to sell. He said that if my father agreed to pay full price for anything, there had to be some deal in the works, and he wasn't going to budge until he found out what. My dad was furious."

According to Sherman, Eleazar Troup attended City Council meetings solely for the chance to call Harley Grove a slumlord in public. "What did your father ever do to him?"

Sherman slowed down a little. "Nothing, so far. I think it's . . . I don't know. Maybe it's a matter of style. My dad's young, with all his hair and teeth and muscles. He jogs and plays tennis and he looks great. Even his shirts are made to order. He was elected to the City Council on his first try. We live in a big house, and we have two new cars. Mr. Troup is old and shriveled and he walks as if his bones hurt. His house is all he owns in the world. My mom is always mentioned in the society pages, and his only kid is a reporter on a dumb local newspaper."

10

I didn't point out that the society pages were in the same local newspaper. I could see what Sherman meant, though. If you had an only child who was a surgeon or a judge, you'd have at least some reflected sense of importance. Personally, I thought it would be more interesting to be a reporter, but there aren't many rich, famous reporters outside of television.

"My father says Pat Troup is the best newsperson in the state," I observed.

My father didn't really know Pat Troup—just enough to say hello when he happened to see her coming to or from her dad's. She was in her early twenties, not much over five feet tall, with a round face and big, nearsighted dark brown eyes. The plastic lenses of her heavy-rimmed glasses were always scratched, and everything I'd ever seen her wear looked left over from Dr. Who's garage sale. Even her short, black curly hair looked like Dr. Who's.

Pat's father wasn't on speaking terms with any of my family. When we first moved in, he made it clear he was dubious about having children and animals next door. Of course, there's a built-in probability that three kids and three dogs are going to do things to upset a less-than-friendly neighbor. I suspect we were much of the reason he put his house up for sale.

My father tried to tell us Mr. Troup was selling because he didn't need the space after Pat got married. She had a big wedding, but a few weeks later,

Cheryl Fabares, who had been a high school class-mate of Pat's new husband, Sonny, came back for a visit. Cheryl had been a pom-pom, girl and high school homecoming queen and a junior fashion model at Lowering's Department Store downtown.

A few days after Cheryl arrived, Sonny told Pat their marriage had been a mistake.

After the divorce, Pat lost a lot of weight, and was shifted to writing obituaries, probably because she had started crying at awkward times. Lately she'd gained back her weight and was covering the news again, but she didn't move home with her father.

I knew the whole story just from overhearing talk around the school lockers. Some of the girls had big sisters who actually knew the people involved personally. The story had passion, betrayal, shame, everything. "She should have known, marrying a younger man," Marti Dunnigan said solemnly. Kerri White pointed out that Sonny was only a couple of years younger than Pat, but everybody around the locker sided with Marti, probably because that made it all the more poignant. Teena Brannigan, who had the lead in the first school play of the season, kept saying, "She must be devastated."

I was impressed, myself, with how brave Pat was to stay in town and keep working on the paper when she knew everybody was feeling sorry for her or saying she should have known better than to marry a younger man.

I could feel for Mr. Troup, too. It must hurt to see your grown child suffering when she's too old to cry on your lap.

As we walked in the front door of our school, I thought about my own family's problems again. "Sherman, it sounds to me as if, no matter what we do, we're likely to end up with no place to live."

"Well . . . whatever happens, you get thirty days' notice. That's the law." He turned down the left-hand corridor to his locker.

I knew, of course, he'd find me at lunch, just as I knew he'd walk home with Aida and me. This day, though, I was grateful. So long as Sherman kept analyzing the problem, it kept me busy thinking about it, rather than simply fretting.

There's hardly a minute or a place in junior high school that doesn't relate to your social status.

Lunchtime sums it all up. At the peak of security are the people who know beforehand not only with whom they'll sit, but where. Each table is like a separate colony, with some clustered like federations. If I had the nerve, I would make this observation in social studies.

There are the tables where the most popular people sit, and the tables taken by the fairly popular, and tables where people stick together out of self-protection. Then there are outskirt tables, with a lot of empty seats.

There are rules for lunchtime loners. You never

sit at a table occupied by people who always eat together. You avoid tables with couples who look as if
they want to be left alone. When you pick a table,
you leave at least one empty chair on either side of
you so nobody will think you're pushy.

When Sherman got to lunch ahead of me, he had
no trouble saving me a seat. When he arrived after
me, there was always an empty chair next to me.

If Sherman had already found a table, he'd wave
to me, and I'd go sit with him. You can't ignore
somebody who has saved you a seat and is franti-
cally waving. Besides, if I did, he'd probably come
to wherever I was sitting and ask why I was mad.

This day, I looked for him as I entered. All morning, I'd been thinking about how much trouble we
had had finding a place to rent when we'd moved to
town. Then, when Mr. Grove was going to evict us,
my father had spent every weekend and evening
searching for another place that would take three
children and three dogs.

He never found one.

I joined Sherman at a table where two other people were trying to look absorbed in what they were
eating.

I could always tell the mood of the Groves' maid
by the lunches Sherman brought. New maids
usually packed him sandwiches with the crust
trimmed off, the tomatoes sliced thin, olives or
pickles drained and isolated in foil or leakproof
bags, cakes or pastries in little plastic boxes, and
maybe a thermos full of soup or hot chocolate.

Their current maid's morale was falling. On Monday, he'd brought hors d'oeuvres, mixed nuts, and garnishes left over from his parents' weekend entertaining. Tuesday, she sent him to school with a lunch of leftover clam dip and no chips.

I unwrapped my sandwich. "There could be some other reason your father wants to show your uncle our house."

"I hope so, Dez."

"I guess the safest thing to do is fix up the place, though."

"I guess." Here it was near the end of the week, and instead of pickles or olives with his sandwich, Sherman had four cocktail onions, stained in various pastel shades where the party toothpicks had been stuck in them.

"Besides," I said, "my father will see that we do." The more I talked, the more depressed I felt.

"You want my cashews?" Sherman asked.

I shook my head.

t w o

Sherman never waited for me at my locker after school. I think he found Kerri and Marti overwhelming. Besides having skipped a grade, he was small for his age, and they towered over him.

He was waiting at the exit this afternoon, as usual.

We walked to Aida's school. She came out alone, in the wake of clusters of laughing, talking little girls.

"You want to come by my house?" Sherman asked after we'd all walked a block. "I taped Bruce Springsteen's new video."

Aida looked up at me, but I said, "We can't. The house, remember?"

"Probably the best video he's ever made," Sherman said.

"Well . . . just to see that one. Then we've got to get home and start working."

Sherman was right. It was a great video. Afterward, he played a whole string of Springsteen videos, from the concert clip of "Rosalita," before The Boss had muscles, through the ones where he got older and stronger. Even a strange, wimpy kid like Sherman can understand what this macho-looking, New Jersey–talking guy is singing about. My sister understood that "Born in the U.S.A." and "My Hometown" were very serious. She watched solemnly and respectfully.

By the time I remembered we were supposed to go right home from school, I had to run all the way, dragging poor Aida, furious with myself for getting us into trouble.

Though Mrs. Farisee was grim, she wasted only a few minutes castigating us. Antony had already hauled a great pile of junk out from under the bunk bed, and Aida and I went to work, chastened.

One thing about Mrs. Farisee, she dealt with a situation when it came up, rather than save it for our father. She didn't mention anything about our being late when he got home for dinner.

By the time I'd finished my homework that evening, he had cleaned the kitchen and bathroom grouting and reattached a sofa arm. He was beginning to replace the broken light switch inside the front door.

I held the flashlight for my father and told him about Sherman's analysis of why Harley Grove wanted to show Bramwell Grove our house.

"The kid's fantastic," my father said, lining up the switch plate.

"You mean he's right?"

"I have lived in rentals most of my life. I can guarantee you he's right." He screwed the plate onto the wall.

"He's not even twelve yet."

"He watches. He listens. He's an outsider." My father tested the new switch, and it worked.

"He is also generally known as a wimp."

My father sat on the sofa, careful not to lean on the arm. "I'm sure he is. I'm willing to bet that nobody comes looking for his company, or chooses him for a team, or asks his opinion. If his parents listened when he yowled in his crib, they haven't heard him since. He has time to watch and think without anybody tampering with his ideas."

Our dog Sadie got up and strolled over to lean against my father's leg. He scratched her behind the ears absentmindedly. "Fortunately, Sherman is a gentle soul. A highly intelligent wimp who cherishes grievances or has a brittle conscience means big trouble. If he goes establishment, he sits at a big table advising others how to inflict maximum casualties on an enemy or a competitor."

Herb and Joe, our male dogs, crowded in between Sadie and my father. Dogs don't waste time fussing. Sadie came and sprawled across my legs, now that I was lying on the floor.

My father scratched Herb and Joe around their necks. "If we're luckier than we deserve, wimps

18

grow up to produce harmless and dazzling technologies or theories or cures, and all the jocks and cheerleaders who ignored them pretend they were their best friends in school."

He stopped scratching. Herb and Joe gave him a minute to start again. When he didn't, they came and flopped down by me. Herb rested his head on Sadie's side, and Joe planted his great paws across my feet.

All three dogs are large and shaggy and prone to shedding. Herb looks like an Old English sheepdog, with some Labrador retriever and beagle thrown in. Joe seems to be mainly Newfoundland, with a bit of collie and Belgian sheepdog. Sadie may well be a mix of vizsla, German shepherd, and Gordon setter. Whatever they are, they're sociable, even when they're not moving.

It's comforting to be around mellow animals and a parent in a conversational mood.

"Steven Spielberg was a wimp in high school," my father said. "So was Stephen King, which is undoubtedly where he got stories like *Carrie*. So was Bruce Springsteen."

I sat up. I love my father. I respect my father. But there are some things you cannot accept, even from a parent. "No. No. Not Bruce Springsteen. Bruce Springsteen was never a wimp."

"I read it somewhere. He said he was really out of it all through high school. What do you think his song 'Glory Days' is all about? It's about those high school cheerleaders and baseball stars passing

19

thirty, selling cars or working in little offices, and dreaming of their glory days, or of lives like the wimps have made for themselves."

Being a psychologist, my father studied these things. Being a psychologist instead of a psychiatrist, he works for salary in a little office at an underfunded community health clinic. He was a marriage counselor before my mother walked out on us. He lost a lot of clients then, and, before he got the job he has now, he sold cars for a while.

For a second, I thought that if he'd ever seen the video he'd know it was about a high school baseball player who ends up a construction worker. Then I realized that even if he'd seen the video, which wasn't likely, the song would still be, to him, about the kind of dead end closest to him. That's why he hadn't mentioned any female wimps.

From what he'd told me about his high school days, my father hadn't been totally out of it, but I knew without asking that his glory days, however long gone, had never been that great.

He is over forty, and the Springsteens and Spielbergs and Kings had been freshmen when he was a graduating senior.

I sat there, my legs pinned down by dogs, and wondered what I'd do if I had the choice of taking my glory now and having it over by thirty, or being what I am now in order to have a dazzling life later.

I didn't even try to imagine Mike Harbinger being less than terrific at thirty. That was unthinkable.

Meanwhile, there was the other immediate, burning issue. "Out of it is one thing. But not a wimp. Never. Not Bruce Springsteen."

I woke at dawn on Thursday. My father was out trimming hedges and cutting what grass our dogs had spared. Before he left for work, he called Shirley Miller and broke their date for that night, which was sad. He wouldn't be seeing her all weekend, since he was leaving for the mental health convention Friday.

While Shirley was probably not in her glory days, I thought I wouldn't mind being like her when I grow up.

That was the trouble with Shirley. I not only liked and admired her, I couldn't help thinking, in spite of myself, about how it might be if my father married her.

He could hardly expect her to share his Hide-A-Bed sofa in the parlor. Nor could they move into one of the bedrooms and shift Mrs. Farisee or the twins and me to the parlor. The pantry was too small to sleep three kids, and Mrs. Farisee would never consent to being moved in there.

If my father married Shirley, Mrs. Farisee would have to go. Shirley would never object to dogs in the house—she always wrestled around with ours when she came over. Shirley would not only let you go to a Saturday matinee before you cleaned your room, she'd probably come with you.

At the same time, I felt creepy thinking of another woman, even Shirley, moving into our house and into the center of my father's life. Worse, I was ashamed that such thoughts could sneak into my mind when I already had a mother.

The most awful thought was that my mother might decide she wanted to come back, after my father had married Shirley.

He did not try to push Mrs. Farisee to do more than her usual work. Instead, he switched around his afternoon appointments so that he was home by the time we got in from school.

The man had no qualms about pushing his own children. He set the twins to washing the bottoms of the windows while I cleaned the tops.

The floors filled him with despair, a despair which Mrs. Farisee felt duty bound to deepen.

"Wax," she declared, "will never restore the surface."

"They didn't look so great when we moved in," I reminded my father.

"And months of dog claws and tracked-in dirt have done them no good." Mrs. Farisee was speaking of the days when she had not been around. Not even the Mongol hordes would track dirt into a house where she ruled. "You'll have to refinish them."

My father rushed out to rent a machine that stripped and waxed floors.

Mrs. Farisee went to a movie so she wouldn't be present for the operation.

My father sent the twins and me out into the yard with the dogs, warning us to keep moving so we wouldn't get chilled. Then he moved furniture, stripped the parts of the floor that showed, and put down a Varathane finish.

He took the twins and me with him to return the machine, and to a drive-in for dinner. By that time he was too exhausted to muster even a roar when Aida, reaching over his shoulder to appropriate the last of his French fries, spilled vanilla milkshake down his neck.

The next morning he overslept, and rushed to work without eating.

"The man is a wreck already," I told Sherman as we walked to school, "and your uncle hasn't even set foot in the house."

My father came home from work with just enough time to throw his things into a suitcase. Mrs. Farisee drove him to the airport. She didn't let us come. "Your father," she said, "is not up to a car full of children."

Left home with strict orders to keep the twins in, the dogs out, the doors locked, and the house neat, I turned on the television in the parlor. Watching my father's set instead of wrangling with the twins over programs was a luxury. Then I got to thinking about all the families in town who had cable.

I found a spy movie set in the Caribbean. While the hero and a beautiful mysterious woman were being stalked through streets clogged with conga dancers and steel-drum bands, our telephone rang. I brought it into the parlor.

It was Sherman. "They're talking condos," he announced.

"Combos?" I kept my eyes on the television screen.

"Condos. My father was just on the phone to Bramwell. The deal is, my dad's pushing the City Council to rezone your neighborhood."

I turned down the set. From the bedroom, I heard the continuing beat of the steel-drum band. I knew I shouldn't let the twins watch a movie that might turn violent, but I had more serious worries.

"Right now, they can only build single-family houses on your block." Sherman's voice was low, like that of somebody calling the police from a public telephone. "See, he plans to sell the houses he owns on your block to my uncle, then get the planning commission to condemn the block, so my uncle can tear down the houses and build condominiums. It won't look good if my father owns all the houses and pushes through the rezoning while he's on the City Council, and then builds the condos. It will look even worse if he gets elected mayor next fall. I'm not sure it would be legal."

I heard the twins opening and closing cupboard doors, but I couldn't even yell at them not to make a mess. Sherman's news had hit me like a poison-tipped blow dart.

He went on in that same guarded voice. "No condo in the world is going to take a family with

24

three dogs, let alone three the size of Herb and Joe and Sadie. From what I gather, my dad expects no trouble in getting the properties condemned, since the city is all gung ho for redevelopment. The eviction process, though, may take a while, especially if Mr. Troup refuses to sell or go quietly. He'll have the time of his life holding everything up."

"Sherman, what are we going to do?"

He was quiet for a long time. Then he murmured, "I don't know, Dez."

We went on talking for a while, but he came up with nothing hopeful. Since his parents had just gone out and their maid was watching television, he didn't really have to worry about being overheard.

When I heard a distinctive engine rattle outside, I hung up and turned off the spy movie and brushed hair and cracker crumbs off the Hide-A-Bed sofa and shooed the dogs into the backyard. Then I went back to our bedroom to be sure the twins hadn't done anything to get me in trouble.

They were making their own steel-drum band out of some empty cans. "Be sure there aren't any sharp edges," I warned.

Mrs. Farisee stuck her head in our bedroom door, said, "I'm back and stop that banging," and went to the kitchen to start dinner.

I helped her. I didn't tell her what Sherman had said. Knowing how she focused on the worst, I was sure she'd have me convinced we'd all be out on the street by Christmas.

After dinner, the twins and I washed dishes, and

then Mrs. Farisee set me to my homework even though it was Friday night.

After I finished, I washed my hair. Mrs. Farisee always said that going to bed with a wet head would bring on pneumonia. I figured, what did I have to lose? Even Harley Grove and his brother Bramwell would hesitate to evict a family with a kid recovering from pneumonia, if that kid had once been in the paper for rescuing the landlord's own flesh and blood.

I poured about a quarter-cup from the shampoo bottle over my head, thinking that maybe in the morning I'd go buy a magazine that had hairstyles in it.

It would be neat, I thought, to have a friend to try out hairdos with. We might even admit to each other that we wanted to look older because of Mike Harbinger. We might even share daydreams about him.

It took a minute for me to realize that I had a serious problem. My hair was sticking to my hands. I tried rinsing my hair, but that seemed to make it gummy. Then it started to get stiff.

Mrs. Farisee banged on the bathroom door and told me to stop wasting hot water. I wrapped a towel around my head, and actually went to her for help.

It was a struggle pulling the towel off and even then some of the fuzz stuck to my hair.

While I tried to drag a comb through the tangles,

Mrs. Farisee went to the bathroom and came back with the shampoo bottle. "I threw this in the wastebasket empty this morning. Where did you get it?"

"It was by the sink. Mrs. Farisee, the comb is caught in my hair."

It took two of us to free the comb, and then I was barely able to get my hands off my head.

Mrs. Farisee strode into the bedroom, where the twins were watching "Friday Night Chillers" with the sound off. She turned off the picture and interrogated them.

Since they had no idea they'd done anything wrong, they freely admitted that they'd used the polyurethane tin for their steel-drum band. They had even saved the last of the stuff by pouring it into the empty shampoo bottle, which they had left by the sink.

They were fascinated by the results, watching silently as Mrs. Farisee and I tried everything from vinegar to salad oil on my hair as the Varathane hardened.

She even turned up the water heater so I could try to shampoo with regular hand soap.

Finally, she said I'd have to use her hair dryer before exhaustion guaranteed me pneumonia. When I finished using the dryer, she came into the bathroom with a green-and-orange paisley print scarf of hers. "Here. Tie up your head so you don't catch a draft. We'll think of something in the morning."

three

In the morning, all she could think of was professional help.

Sherman had come over early, as he usually did.

"Oh, wow, Dez," he breathed, gazing at my hair. Instead of lying flat, it stood up in clumps and spikes, probably because I'd spent a restless night.

Sherman, of course, had known me from the time my hair had just started coming back. After my mother left, my hair had fallen out until I had a little bald spot on top. The psychologist my father sent me to said it was from stress, and in time my hair did grow in. I suppose Sherman felt it was especially poignant that it had returned only to be Varathaned.

"There has got to be something made that will dissolve this guck," I said, trying hard not to cry.

"Varnish remover," Mrs. Farisee said, "and it would peel the scalp right off you."

"You try any more stuff on your head, Dez,"

Sherman agreed, "and you might get some really weird chemical reaction."

The twins edged closer, obviously hoping that I might bring about a reaction so spectacular it would make their Saturday.

"Of course, I don't know any beauty shop that will take you without an appointment on a weekend." Mrs. Farisee always felt obliged to mention the worst possible outcome.

I got out the telephone book anyway, and leafed through the yellow pages, half afraid Mrs. Farisee might offer to take me to the beauty shop she used. Her hair lay in still, perfect curls, like a colony of ghostly lavender-tinted snail shells.

Sherman, looking over my shoulder, put his finger on the Mona Lisa Salon ad. "That's in the Rancho Grande Mall. My uncle Bramwell owns the whole mall."

"Tell them," Mrs. Farisee suggested. "You might get a discount."

I telephoned the Mona Lisa and explained that it was an emergency, but I couldn't bring myself to mention Bramwell Grove.

After all, it was partly due to him and his condo plans that my head was polyurethaned.

I got an appointment for ten o'clock.

Mrs. Farisee said I could not go to a beauty shop wearing jeans, so I went to the bedroom to change. The twins took their ant farm into the kitchen to show Sherman.

29

My mother had sent it to them for their birthday.

My mother had always had a feeling for animals. She had rescued more than I could count, pulling off the freeway to help some crazed lanky hound out of the traffic, squatting in the rain in a downtown parking lot to coax a half-wild, terrified cat to her.

Then she left us—to find herself, she explained.

When she left, she was a person who would not have a mousetrap in the house. Whoever she had found had given her own kids a bunch of ants sealed in plastic.

I didn't want to think about what had happened to her, but I couldn't stop. Either she had changed, or she had sold out to be like everybody else, or she was so busy she remembered the birthday at the last minute and just bought anything without considering. To buy an ant farm, though, meant she had changed.

There was the other possibility. Maybe she hadn't taken time to buy it herself, but had asked somebody to pick out a present for her kids. Maybe some boyfriend had selected it and even mailed it for her.

Thinking about her and that ant farm hurt so much I hoped she'd just forget my birthday.

Antony and Aida watched the ant farm sometimes, maybe because it was a present from their mother, but you can't get thrilled about a bunch of trapped ants.

I felt under the bunk bed for my left shoe. How

can you clean your room and still lose a shoe? I wondered. I rummaged through the wastebasket and dresser drawers, until the room began to look as it had before we cleaned it.

While I was standing on a chair feeling over the closet shelf, I heard Sherman worrying aloud about how the ants must feel spending their lives in a plastic prison.

Nobody else had had the heart to tell the twins what a monstrous thing the farm was.

Before he could upset Antony and Aida too much, I yelled, "Sherman! Look in the parlor and see if my shoe is under anything."

I began tossing stuff out of the twins' toy box, even though I knew I'd have to put it all back. As I hauled out dirty socks, crumpled paper, gum wrappers, and parts of toys, I heard Antony in the kitchen.

"Wait. Wait. Wait," he said urgently. "You can't just turn them loose without anything to eat."

Right away, I knew what was going on.

I hurried into the kitchen with my right shoe untied. Antony was taking a jar of honey from the refrigerator. Aida stood holding the farm and weeping quietly, I suppose at the prospect of parting with the ants.

"Would a chewed-up thong do?" Sherman yelled from the parlor.

"You've got to take it well away from the house," I told the twins, "and then pry it open without hurting them. They'll need just a spoonful of

31

honey." I went out to the back porch and looked for a screwdriver.

There was a wail from the kitchen, and a crash. I ran back in time to see Antony run to the fridge and stick his wet, scalded hand into the freezer compartment.

Hot water was still running over the broken honey jar in the sink. A few ants were beginning to leak out of the farm Aida had dropped when Antony scalded his hand.

"What is going on in here?" Mrs. Farisee came rushing in from her room.

I started to explain that Antony had been trying to soften the honey by running hot water over the jar, when he let out another yowl. By then, of course, his hand was stuck firmly to the freezer wall.

While Herb and Joe and Sadie scratched at the back door and howled to come in, Mrs. Farisee disconnected the refrigerator and we poured warm water over my brother's hand to thaw him loose. Sherman and Aida looked on, awed and silent.

The scalded part of Antony's hand was red and puffy, with dead white frostbite in the center. Mrs. Farisee carried him out to my father's car while I ran after her with her purse. "Remember your hair appointment," she told me as she belted Antony in. *"And get rid of those ants!"*

I herded my sister back into the house, Sherman following.

As we squatted in the kitchen, watching the ants spill out of the cracked farm, Sherman said, "Boy.

Not many kids his age can scald and freeze themselves at the same time."

"It's not easy to run hot water over something you're holding without running hot water over your hand," I pointed out. "And I used so much on my hair last night that Mrs. Farisee turned up the water heater."

"How are we going to catch the ants without hurting them?" Aida asked.

"There's got to be a way," I said.

"Bags!" Sherman said. "Plastic bags!"

Since it was his idea, I made him pick up the ant farm while I held the plastic trash bag. Being, as my father had noted, a gentle soul, Sherman couldn't wash off the ants that swarmed up his fingers. With Aida trailing him anxiously, he ran outside and tried to shake free of them. While Aida begged him not to hurt the ants, the dogs barked and jumped on him delightedly.

By the time Sherman and my sister came in, I'd put a second and third bag over the first, securing each tightly.

"How are they going to breathe?" Aida was already pale and teary from Antony's ordeal.

"There is enough air in there for ants," I assured her. "Trust me. Believe me."

"What about the ants loose in the kitchen?"

"First, we've got to do something with the whole farm. Then we'll come back and find a good home for the stragglers."

"What about the broken jar?"

"Aida, ants are too small to get cut on glass. They are too small to swallow glass. This has been scientifically proven."

I went back to our room to look for my shoe. Whatever happened, I could not be late to the Mona Lisa. You don't wrangle a Saturday appointment by pleading emergency and then arrive late. Not only would I be turned away, the receptionist might not be able to work me in for days. Meanwhile, moment by moment, polyurethane might be penetrating my scalp and destroying my brain.

To get to the Mona Lisa, I had to go out in public. Baring my hair was unthinkable. I looked around for the scarf Mrs. Farisee had loaned me. I ransacked the room again.

Then I had a moment's good sense. I pulled down my bedspread. The scarf was still on my pillow.

I looked under the pillow for my shoe, but that was expecting too much. Taking off my right shoe, I padded out to the back porch and put on my rain boots. These were not fashion boots. These were strictly for storms, so clunky you would never want to be seen on the street in them unless the skies had already opened.

But no one would be looking at my feet.

For all her tender feelings, my sister has a practical streak. She had ferreted out half a dozen soda bottles and put them in the wagon with the ant bags. "I'll trade them in to buy comic books," she explained.

"You want me to come with you?" Sherman asked me.

"You? *You?*" Then I saw how anxious and miserable he looked. There was no point in reminding him that but for his relatives, but for his own talk of stir-crazy ants, none of these catastrophes would have happened. Once I got started, I might get so carried away I'd make myself late to the Mona Lisa. "I think you'd better go home," I told him, as calmly as I could.

He plugged in the refrigerator and left.

So, at twelve and a half, an age when merely being seen in the wrong cut of jeans can ruin you socially, I had to walk all the way to the Rancho Grande Mall looking like a refugee from a Latvian potato farm, with my little sister pulling a wagon full of ants and bottles.

At her best, Aida resembled a bag lady in training. Mrs. Farisee, in her early weeks as our housekeeper, had been determined to keep Aida presentable. This was like trying to hold back a glacier. Slowly, inexorably, from the time she bathed and combed and dressed herself in the morning, my sister began accumulating skinned knees, rips, and tangles in a general decline toward total grubbiness.

The Rancho Grande Mall was a rundown shopping center a dozen blocks from our house, in a neighborhood of service stations and World War Two tract houses, with no place where we could leave an ant colony without being noticed.

Between a coin-operated laundry and a shoe-repair shop was a wide display window with *Mona Lisa Salon de Beauté* swirled in pink script across it, and a glass door with a sign that read *Open Evenings, Appointments Not Necessary.*

"You'll have to leave the wagon outside," I told my sister.

"I'll stay here with it," she said.

I don't know whether she was worried that some wagon-napper might swoop by, or whether she wanted to be with the ants as long as possible, but I was relieved.

"Then you stay right by the window," I told her sternly. "You do not move an inch, and you do not speak to a soul."

She nodded.

I knew she would obey my orders to the letter. After the morning we'd had, she wouldn't dare provoke me.

I slunk into the Mona Lisa Salon.

A stocky woman with blue eye shadow sat at the front desk reading *Soap Opera Digest*. Her hair looked like the spun glass that fancy department stores use for clouds in Christmas displays.

"My name is Desdemona Blank," I said. "I have an appointment with Miss Lisa."

Flicking me with a quick glance, she dismissed me as nobody to respect. She put down the magazine and stood, pulling down the skirt of her shiny pink nylon uniform. "Okay. Come on."

36

To establish some kind of relationship, I added, "I'm a friend of Bramwell Grove's nephew."

The woman sat down again. "Mona!" she yelled. "You take this one."

"I think the appointment was with Miss Lisa," I reminded her, thinking she had been absorbed in her reading when I first said it.

"I'm going to be booked up."

A woman in an almost identical pink uniform and hair like cotton candy came from behind a curtain at the rear of the shop, advancing with heavy step and narrowed eyes. "Whataya mean, take this one? Isn't this your ten o'clock?"

"You take this one and I'll close up tonight."

Mona gazed at me with all the cheer of somebody reading a midwinter utility bill.

"I wonder if you could put me kind of near the back, but where I could still see out the window," I ventured.

Mona steered me to the closest chair. "Take off the kerchief."

I didn't want to lose both Mona and Lisa with my hair still varnished, so I sat down and untied the scarf.

"Wha ... she's shellacked!" Mona cried. "Lisa, look at this!"

Lisa sidled around the desk and, standing beside Mona, gingerly poked my hair with an enameled fingernail. "It's solid."

Mona was stern. "Kid, this may seem like a ter-

rific new fad to you, but, believe me, you're wreck-
ing your hair varnishing it."

"I didn't. My brother and sister—"

"They *varnished* you?" Mona demanded.

Turning her head away from me slightly, Lisa
muttered to Mona, "Friends of Bram Grove."

"My father refinished the floors," I explained.
"When my brother and sister used the varnish tin
to make a drum, they emptied the Varathane into a
shampoo bottle and left it in the bathroom."

Mona and Lisa asked no more questions, but con-
ferred about the remedy for my condition. Everything Mona suggested, Lisa vetoed. Everything Lisa
came up with, Mona rejected. Aida kept glancing in,
troubled by their growing vehemence.

"We got to go trial and error here," Mona declared finally, and finally Lisa agreed.

They sprayed my hair with hot water. It ran off
my head like rain from a tile roof. They tried to
massage in shampoo and gel and creme and mousse,
but my hair remained solid and impervious.

Mona and Lisa got sweaty and flushed and more
snappish. Every few minutes, Aida peered in, but
the atmosphere was so tense she didn't dare step
inside.

Finally Mona and Lisa became calm, like death-
row cellmates who realize they're stuck with each
other. Withdrawing to the rear of the shop, they
caucused urgently, whispering at each other more
and more vehemently.

When they came back, they looked at me in the

mirror, and then Mona said, "Honey, there's no way around it. The hair has got to go."

With the two of them agreeing, I knew they had to be right.

I wanted desperately to grab the scarf and run out of there, but I knew my father and Mrs. Farisee would never let me walk around with floor finish on my head.

Mona and Lisa began wrangling even more hotly over the *way* to cut my hair. Finally, Mona went across the mall to the television repair shop and borrowed a couple of screwdrivers. She used them like chopsticks, working them through my hair to pry a chunk free and hold it up while Lisa cut it off.

Closing my eyes, I forced myself to sit without a whimper, without a shudder, as each lock struck my shoulders or clunked on the floor. I knew that any movement might destroy Lisa's concentration.

At last she said, "If we cut any more you'll look like a loofah. Tell your mother—"

"My mother's . . . away." I opened my eyes, but I was careful not to look at a mirror.

"Tell your father that when it grows out you'll look—"

"Better," Mona said.

"Somewhat," Lisa added. "Tell him we did the best we could and there's no sense him coming in here making a scene."

"He won't. He's traveling."

I tied on the scarf, unable to look at Mona and Lisa.

I was at the desk, counting out money for Mona, when I heard Sherman's voice outside. "Hey, Aida. Dez in there?"

Sherman entered with a man who sauntered in like a movie star arriving for a press conference. Tall, with thick, glossy black hair and dark eyes, he was handsome in a tense way, faintly menacing like the heroes on the covers of the paperback romances Mrs. Farisee bought at the supermarket. He wore a black, double-breasted cashmere overcoat, black gloves, dark trousers, a silky scarf, and supple black shoes.

"I got a ride with my uncle," Sherman greeted me.

It is not easy to discourage a wimp who is devoted to you.

Sherman's uncle ignored me. "So, Lisa, how's it going?"

"Business is terrible and I'm Mona." Her voice was flat and wary.

"Whatever. The rent check you told me was in the mail last week never came."

"We didn't count on your hiking the rent twice in a year," Lisa told him.

"Everybody's got to live, ladies. I can't support the world."

"We haven't cleared three hundred this week," Mona said.

"I'll take it now, cash, the balance next week."

When adults are talking like this, the best thing

40

to do is pretend you don't understand. I studied the pictures of hairstyles on the walls.

Mona and Lisa collected cash from the register and their handbags and Bramwell took it and said he'd return in a week. Aiming a pat at Sherman's head, he told him, "See ya, kid," and strode from the salon.

Mona took my money and counted out my change in dimes and quarters. "So your father's a traveling salesman and your uncle's—"

"No, no," I corrected her hastily. "That's *Sherman's* uncle."

"Try to take after the other side of your family," Mona advised him.

Aida stuck her head in the door. "Can we do something about my ants now?"

"If your aunts are related to Bram Grove, don't recommend this place to them," Lisa told me.

Sherman followed me from the salon. "So let's see how they fixed your hair."

"It looked as if they were cutting it to the *skin*," Aida said.

"Take her to trade in the bottles," I told Sherman.

Aida hauled the wagon across the street to the market, talking steadily to Sherman. I sat on the edge of a concrete planter box, under a stunted, leafless tree. Feeling the cold wind through my scarf, I put my head down so that nobody would notice if I started to cry.

41

Sherman and Aida were gone so long I knew she was either reading all the comics on the racks or stalled over which to buy.

While I was deciding whether to go get her, she came out of the supermarket with Sherman and crossed the parking lot, pulling the wagon and shaking carob chips out of a bag into her mouth. I knew she'd bought them because they were cheap, being sold in bulk. It was too late to wonder how many other kids had had their hands in the bin.

"Watch out for cars, dummy!" I yelled.

There I was, sitting on a planter box with my head tied up in a kerchief, which probably did not hide the fact that I was nearly bald. I was yelling in a voice like an elephant seal's at my sister, who was pulling a wagon full of ant farm and shaking carob chips into her face while crossing a parking lot. With her was our landlord's eleven-year-old wimp son, my best friend in the world.

And there were Mike Harbinger and his friends, not twenty feet away, looking at me.

The wind whipped a hamburger wrapper across the lot and tugged at the back point of my scarf.

Holding down the kerchief, I dashed over to grab Aida and hurry away from Mike Harbinger.

"What about my ants?" Aida kept asking me. "What about the ants?"

"You can't bring them home, Dez," Sherman warned.

We were at the very margin of the mall before I stopped. On our left was a raised rectangular island landscaped with rocks and juniper. I nodded toward it. "They've got to live outside, Aida, or somebody is sure to spray them or stomp them."

Shoving the chips into her coat pocket, Aida climbed up on the planter, clutching the trash bags.

"Hey." Bramwell Grove came out the back door of the bakery. "What are you dumping in there?"

Sherman was too taken aback to start with a good explanation and then work up gradually to the answer. "Ants."

Bramwell Grove was more formidable than most adults. Instead of looking blank, or surprised, he exploded instantly. "Ants? Live ants? You're putting live ants in my mall?"

"Harmless ants," I said hastily. "My sister's ant farm is cracked and they're kind of leaking out."

"You don't have a trash can at home?" Bramwell asked coldly.

"We're trying to find the ants a warm, safe place to live," Sherman explained.

Bramwell put a hand on his nephew's shoulder. "Kid, there is no such place."

My sister stood, scared and uncertain, looking up at Bramwell. Aida is not cute, or pert, or cuddly. What Aida is, is sincere.

Bramwell Grove looked down at her. Aida looked up at him. His gaze shifted. Then, sounding exasperated and embarrassed, he growled, "Will you hurry it up, then? You want people to see me hanging out with a bunch of kids that relocate ants?"

Hastily, fumbling, as if afraid he might change his

mind, Aida undid the twist-ties and shook out the plastic bags. Ants crawled onto her like shipwreck survivors onto an island.

I had not realized just how many ants that farm contained.

As she brushed and shook herself, I stood for a second, too astonished to realize she needed rescuing.

Bramwell Grove gazed at the spectacle. "You ever see that Charlton Heston movie where he's in the jungle and millions of army ants go on the march?"

"Yeah," Sherman said. "Like, they strip an elephant to the bones in—"

"For Pete's sake!" Shoving me aside, a woman set her grocery bags on the ledge and leaped onto the island. Even as I recognized Shirley Miller, Sherman jumped up to help her.

The three of us picked ants off Aida, then shook them off our arms, shoes, fingers. Finally Shirley lifted Aida off the island and brushed a few more ants from her coat.

"I don't even want to know why," Shirley said.

It was typical of Shirley that she didn't ask how we came to be dumping ants from a plastic bag into a shopping center. She would assume we had a legitimate reason. "Where's your brother?"

"He froze his hand and Mrs. Farisee rushed him to the hospital," I said.

"First he scalded it under hot water, then he put it in the refrigerator and it stuck to the freezer part." Though I'm certain Sherman would have proposed to Shirley if he'd been sixteen, he was far from dumbstruck in her presence.

She shook her head in sympathy, then looked up at the sky. "You'd better get home before the storm hits. I'd drive you, but my car's in the shop."

Bramwell Grove regarded her with a mixture of respect and interest, like an explorer who has come upon a puzzling but highly advanced civilization. Even in an old raincoat, she looked lean and lithe, and definitely not his type. "Could I give you a lift?" he asked her.

"My uncle Bramwell," Sherman admitted grudgingly.

"Great," Shirley told Bramwell. "I wouldn't want the kids to get caught in the rain—and if these grocery bags get soaked before I make it home, I'm going to be leaving a trail of canned cat food."

She hoisted one of the bags, and as she bent to pick up the other, he lifted it, but he didn't try to relieve her of the one she already had. Smart, I thought. He's already sizing her up. That made me uneasy.

Shirley took Aida's hand, Aida took the wagon handle, and we followed Bramwell to a new, dark blue, long, low car, like something Ricardo Montalban would advertise on television. As Bramwell glanced at Aida's wagon, I was very sure that if Shirley had not been with us, he would never have allowed that wagon near that car.

He rested the bag on the rear bumper, and un-

45

locked the trunk. "Clean off the wagon," he told my sister.

Aida gave the rear wheels a swipe with her coat sleeve.

Meanwhile, I was worrying about whether to accept the ride or get caught in the rain. Sherman, my closest friend, was coming with us, as was Shirley, my father's girlfriend.

This was Sherman's uncle, who owned the mall and might soon own our house.

I was pretty sure all this didn't add up to justification for taking a ride from the man.

As he unlocked the trunk, I edged closer to Shirley and whispered, "Can you ask him to take us home first?"

"Absolutely," she murmured.

Bramwell put the groceries, then the wagon, in the trunk.

Shirley sat in the front with him.

The upholstery in the car was midnight blue crushed velvet, and the dashboard and door panels were inlaid wood. Besides an instrument panel that must have taken weeks to learn, there was a telephone and a sound system. Before he started the engine, Bramwell inserted a cassette into the player on the dash, and then turned the quadraphonic sound down low.

"I've got to pick up some ledgers first," he told Shirley. "Sorry if it's out of your way, but I need them for my next stop."

He drove downtown, through its core to its husk, to streets with karate studios and resale clothing stores, then streets with surplus stores and boarded-over buildings, pawnshops and bail-bond establishments, and finally streets of movie houses with posters he ordered us not to look at.

I knew I would never, whatever the circumstances, take another ride with anybody without getting permission from Mrs. Farisee or my father. I'd been uncertain when I thought Bramwell was taking us right home—and here we were riding through this awful part of town.

"This is a scary neighborhood," Sherman observed.

"Are you kidding? It's a gold mine," his uncle told him.

"This?" Sherman asked.

Bramwell turned the music down even more. "The whole area's condemned. Town's going to tear everything down and build an industrial park. And I own half the buildings. That, kid, is known as foresight."

Though he was addressing Sherman, he seemed to be talking more to Shirley.

On the next street all the structures looked abandoned. Bramwell parked in front of a three-story building. Though slogans had been spray-painted on every wall around it, it stood unmarked.

Bramwell got out. "Back in a second," he told Shirley. "Keep the doors and windows locked."

Shirley gazed after him as he entered the building. "Interesting personality."

"My mother calls him a slumlord," Sherman confided. "She gets all upset when Mr. Troup calls my father that, but I guess in my uncle's case she thinks it fits."

The sidewalks were littered, and the only living creature I saw was a lank and ribby dog that shambled out of the alley. His coat was sparse and patchy, his muzzle grizzled. His gait was unsteady, as if he were trying not to lie down and give up. He had, overall, the look of a dog with a history that would break your heart.

"Find the button that opens the trunk, Dez, and lock the door after me." Ignoring Bramwell's advice, Shirley got out of the car.

As she approached the dog, he crouched to protect his hindquarters and lifted one placating paw, as if to apologize for his existence.

Scrambling into the front seat, I examined the dashboard, trying to decide what would lock the door and open the trunk.

Shirley reached for the dog. He cringed, trembling, but she edged closer, talking all the time, until she touched his head.

Bramwell came out of the building carrying several black ledgers.

"Slow down," Shirley told him quietly. "Open the trunk and see what I've got to feed him. Give me the frozen fruit bars, too. He's probably thirsty."

It's just what my mother would have done, I thought, *at least before the ant farm.*

"This is not a neighborhood to hang around in," Bramwell told Shirley.

"I know," she said. "Not fit for a dog."

He unlocked the trunk and, moving carefully, brought her a box of fruit bars and another of crackers.

She was right. As she broke the bars off their sticks, the dog gulped them desperately. While he ate the crackers with the same urgency, he was too gentle to snap them out of her hands.

Bramwell stood watching her. "Better get going."

She looked up. "Could you keep him overnight while I figure out what to do with him?"

"*Do* with him?"

"You can see he's starving. We'll have to take him—"

"Not in my car."

Shirley stood. "May I use your car phone to call a cab?"

"You think a cabbie's going to come down here for a fare, even if he'd take you with that mutt?"

She walked around to the passenger door. "Dez, you call home and explain that Sherman and his uncle are driving you. Take my groceries into your house, and I'll be there as soon as I can." She walked back to the dog, who had not taken his eyes off her. "Let's go," she told him.

They'd gone only a few steps when Bramwell

strode after them. "You know you can't be out on these streets alone." ·

She kept going, the dog at her side.

Sherman scrambled into the driver's seat and out of the car. Before I could stop her, Aida followed.

This was not an area in which you yelled, or called attention to yourself in any way. Instead of ordering my sister back, I went after her.

"I'm talking to you!" Bramwell caught up with Shirley. "You think that fleabag is any protection in a neighborhood like this?"

"Maybe you'll be kind enough to call the police if I get in trouble—provided you think they'll come down here."

Bramwell stepped in front of her. "You're trying to make me look like some kind of . . ." He hauled Sherman around beside him. "Would I hurt a dog? Tell her."

"Not unless it owed you money."

Bramwell looked down at his nephew appraisingly. "You got your mother's mouth on you, kid."

"I'm not leaving this animal out on the street," Shirley said. "Look at him. You can see every bone in his body."

It was too much for my sister. Squatting beside the dog, she threw her arms around his neck and began crying quietly.

The dog licked her ear.

If there is a man who can stand up to a righteous woman, a starving dog, and a weeping child, I don't want to meet him.

Bramwell looked around the deserted streets as if to challenge anyone watching us. He glanced down at my sister sniffling against the dog's snout. He glared at me, then at Sherman, who shrugged.

"Get in the car, will you?" he growled. "And keep that hound in your lap in case he's not upholstery-broken," he told Shirley.

"Let me hold him," Sherman pleaded. Sherman had a dog of sorts, six pounds of macho canine swagger. Whenever Sherman brought him to our house, Jake was always snarling and insulting Herb and Joe when he wasn't sidling up to Sadie. Being ten or twelve times his size, our three strove to ignore him. They seemed vaguely embarrassed by Jake, as if he might be mistaken for one of their species. I could see how Sherman would be captivated by this mild, sweet-tempered, down-and-out animal.

As we got in the car, Shirley lifted the dog and put him in Sherman's lap. "When you get home, you'd better wash your clothes and take a shower right away."

Bramwell started the engine. "Should I shower my upholstery or just rip it out?"

"Spray it," she said calmly.

Bramwell drove on silently, not even turning on his quadraphonic music. Sherman stroked the dog's head.

Bramwell glanced at them in the rearview mirror. "That mutt's no spring chicken, you know."

Sherman held the dog closer.

51

"Don't get me wrong," Bramwell went on before Shirley could speak. "I got nothing against dogs. When I was little, I wanted one, just like any kid. I was always after my parents to get one, but they wouldn't, because of Harley."

"My father didn't like dogs?" Sherman asked.

"I don't know about like," his uncle said. "He was scared to death of them—froze if so much as a chihuahua came sniffing around him."

That, I thought, explained why Sherman never got a dog when he was little, and why the one his parents finally got him was so tiny.

"It's true what they say, you know," Bramwell added darkly. "Dogs can scent fear. I swear they can. Anyplace we went, they were always after Harley, nosing at his heels, trying to shake hands, all those dumb dog tricks, trying to make up with him. Me, somehow I never had a way with dogs. I always pictured myself with one, maybe a Doberman or a pit bull. But dogs just never seemed to take to me. You know how many times I've been bit trying to pet one? Or they wait until I turn my back and then fang me in the ankle."

"That's sad." Aida's sympathies, which were active to begin with, were getting a heavy workout this day.

"Did you ever have a pet?" Sherman asked.

"I raised Siamese fighting fish for a while. There used to be a lot of money in fighting fish. Now there's a glut on the market. I still think one of

these days I might find a dog I can get along with."
He slid a new cassette into the player on the dashboard.

At the first notes, the stray on Sherman's lap
began to howl.

Bramwell turned off the player. "Where do you
live?" he asked me.

I told him our address, not reminding him that he
might be buying the place.

He didn't even ask Shirley her address, though,
for all he knew, she lived closer.

As we reached our street, Sherman said, "It's a
crummy block, but it would be a shame to change
it. There aren't that many people around able to
pay higher rents."

"People will pay what they have to," Bramwell
said.

"Is your basement still damp?" Sherman asked
me. "That's probably because your house is built on
fill land. This whole block is probably soggy, if you
dig deep enough. It was probably a mistake to build
anything here in the first place."

Sherman has some great qualities.

"I don't know what I'm going to do about this animal." Shirley sounded worried. "I live in a one-
room apartment where even my cat is contraband."

I was afraid she'd ask us to keep the dog. If we
were barely hanging on to our house, one more
beast was all the excuse Harley Grove would need
to kick us out. Even if we hid the dog when he and

Bramwell came to see the house, Bramwell would know, and when it came to business, I suspected Harley Grove was a softie next to Bramwell.

Shirley, of course, knew better than to ask any renters with three animals to take in a fourth, at least not while the landlord's brother was listening. Also, she had met Mrs. Farisee. "Sherman, do you think—"

"Jake would tear right into him. Besides, it took me most of my life to get Jake."

"Tell Antony I hope his hand's okay," Shirley said, as Aida and I got out of the car. "I'd come in, but . . ."

"But that would be holding me up even more," Bramwell said, locking the car door after us.

As Aida and I reached the porch, the rain started.

four

Mrs. Farisee was sitting on the sofa. My brother was beside her sipping hot chocolate from one of our good cups while she held the saucer for him.

She had never before let any of us eat or drink in the parlor.

Antony looked tired and pale. His right hand was bandaged all the way up the wrist. Even Mrs. Farisee looked worn out. While a hurricane could never muss those lavender curls, her blue eyes looked pale and watery and bloodshot.

What surprised me was that my brother was sitting so close to her. She had always seemed to me like a combination housekeeper and warden. Still, in the first hours after my hair was varnished, she'd been my only resource.

"There's some soup and more hot chocolate on the stove," she told us. "The rest of your lunch is in the fridge."

It was the first time she'd ever been so slapdash about meals.

What with relocating the ants and observing Bramwell and meeting Shirley and rescuing the dog, I'd almost forgotten that I was clipped like a Marine recruit. Being in the house with a kerchief on reminded me now, but I didn't take it off. I wasn't ready to face even the reactions of Mrs. Farisee and my own brother.

I poured soup and hot chocolate for myself and Aida, reminding her, as I always did, that there was no need to add sugar to hot chocolate. From the refrigerator, I took our sandwiches, neatly made and wrapped in plastic.

We didn't presume to bring our lunches into the parlor, knowing that if Antony hadn't required emergency medical care, he wouldn't be drinking in there either.

Thinking of my hair had all but destroyed my appetite. After we finished our chocolate and soup, I put my sandwich back in the refrigerator.

We tidied the kitchen and went in to see how our brother was.

The rain had stopped, and through the front window I saw a car pull up at the curb. It was new, and elegant, though not in a class with Bramwell's. A little boy got out and came to our door. When I opened the door, he turned and waved to the driver, and the car pulled away. Turning back to me, he handed me his furled umbrella and began unbuttoning his trench coat. "I'm Preston." He gave no last name, as if "Preston" were all the world needed to know.

It was plain this kid was not selling mints or tickets to a raffle. I felt as if I were caught in the opening of a television series. Had we won him? Had he adopted us? Could he be the child of some millionaire fifth cousins we'd never met, a rich waif who'd run away from home and come to us for shelter?

Preston was not put off by my bewilderment. Balancing with one hand on the doorjamb, he took off his right rain boot, then his left. "Where's Antony?"

"Antony?" I was dumbfounded. Nobody had ever come to visit my brother.

Antony wasn't tall for a five-year-old, but this boy was even shorter. Still, his air of confidence was unsettling. He had dark eyes, a round face, and thick, straight, dark brown hair, impeccably cut.

He even had color-coordinated raingear, not the yellow slicker and red vinyl boots most kindergartners wore. His coat was a camel-color fleece-lined twill. His umbrella and boots were a matched dark brown.

As he lined up his boots on the porch, I turned toward the parlor. "Antony? You know a Preston?"

Antony handed Mrs. Farisee his cup. "Oh, yeah. I forgot. I invited him over."

We knew we were never, never to invite a friend over without permission from Mrs. Farisee. Inasmuch as none of us had gotten to know anybody that well since we came to town, and inasmuch as Mrs. Farisee regarded Sherman as a pest who came with the job, the rule had never been tested.

I suppose Mrs. Farisee figured a scalded frozen hand and a morning at the emergency room excused Antony's forgetting, because she only said, "We don't keep guests standing at the door, Desdemona."

I stepped back and Preston stepped in.

"Wow!" He stared at Antony's bandaged hand. "Wow! What happened?"

"I burned it, then I froze it," Antony told him.

"Wow! How?"

While Antony explained, I took Aida out of the parlor and hung up Preston's coat in the hall closet. My brother seldom said more than ten words in a row to anybody but his sister, and I didn't want to do anything to make him or his guest uncomfortable.

Aida went back to our bedroom and I wandered into the kitchen. Mrs. Farisee had put the teakettle on.

I don't know what it would take to make Preston uncomfortable. I could hear him in the parlor, peppering Antony's narrative with *wow*s. Ten words? My brother was spilling out hundreds.

When Antony finished, Preston said, "You'll probably get in trouble if you get the bandage dirty right away. We'd better play in your room."

As they headed for the bedroom, I heard him ask,

"Why does that girl wear a scarf on her head in the house?"

"Why does she?" Mrs. Farisee asked me.

"Because I don't want to show my hair, even to myself."

"Sooner or later you'll have to." She set out two cups and put a chamomile tea bag in each. "Take it off. You look foolish."

One doesn't say no to Mrs. Farisee. I untied the scarf, folded it, and put it on the table.

She gazed at my head. "Oh." She took her aspirin bottle off the shelf over the stove and shook out a couple of pills, which she set on one of the saucers. "Well."

It would have been easier if she'd laughed.

The kettle shrieked and she poured hot water into the cups, put them on the saucers, and brought them to the table. Sitting down heavily, she slid the sugar bowl toward me.

While I was waiting for my tea to cool, she popped the aspirins into her mouth and washed them down. Even in a time of stress, she did not gulp.

Aida wandered into the kitchen. Having already seen my shearing in process, she barely glanced at my hair.

"Did they kick you out of the bedroom?" I asked her.

Aida shook her head. "They don't care where I go."

Mrs. Farisee did not permit us to eat between

meals, but now she said, "Why don't you take an apple?"

My sister shook her head.

"How come," I heard Preston ask, "you have three beds in one room?"

"Three of us sleep in here," Antony said.

"Three?"

"My sisters and I."

"Wow! I never shared a room with anybody."

"You want to see my butterfly collection?"

"No." Preston was firm. "I think it's really rotten to catch butterflies."

"I don't mean live butterflies. You think I'd go around catching live *butterflies*? That's *gross*."

"I don't want to see a bunch of dead ones, either. That's even grosser."

"I build them," Antony explained.

My brother would never torment or trap or catch or kill a living creature. That was one of the fine things about him. I worried, though. How would a kid as self-possessed as this Preston feel about a boy who constructed butterflies from tissue paper, wire, and watercolors?

"Oh, wow!" This *wow* was the most sincere Preston had yet uttered, and Preston had already struck me as a master of the sincere *wow*. "Wow! They are . . . oh, wow! Hey, did you ever build model airplanes?"

"No," Antony confessed.

"Listen, I got this model airplane kit for my

birthday, but my father put it away until I'm old enough not to wreck it. If I could show him one of your butterflies, I bet he'd let us make that plane together."

Sitting at the kitchen table, Aida licked the tip of her finger and picked up sugar grains with it. She didn't even scan the floor for ants to rescue.

After I finished my tea, I went into the bathroom. I shut the door and looked in the mirror.

It was worse than I'd expected. The half-inch reddish-brown stubble on my head stood up like new-mowed grass. My eyes seemed enormous, and my ears looked indecent.

For a minute, I felt like throwing up. Then I sat on the edge of the tub, too desolate to cry.

It would be a long, long time before I walked home by way of the football field again.

I thought about facing school on Monday, but the idea was so inconceivably dreadful, I couldn't imagine how it would be.

I got up. The thing to do was keep moving, keep busy.

I couldn't go into the bedroom and set off another commentary by Preston. I fished a sweatshirt and a pair of jeans out of the clothes hamper, then got my old windbreaker from the hall closet and went back to the kitchen. "I promised Dad I'd finish weeding the backyard," I told Mrs. Farisee. "May I borrow your scarf back?"

"You'd better keep it."

As I tied the scarf on, she said, "Be sure to wear your rain boots, and if it's too raw out, you come back in."

I nodded. *With any luck, the weather will be vile, I thought, and I'll come down with something that will keep me out of school a month, and my family quarantined in this house even longer.*

I'd been working a few minutes when Aida came out, bundled up and booted. She pulled weeds steadily, without talking, only glancing up at our bedroom window now and then.

I don't know how long we'd been outside when Mrs. Farisee opened the back door. "Your father's on the phone."

I pulled off my windbreaker and the scarf as Aida and I came in the back door.

Our telephone was on a small, high table in the hall, where it was impossible to carry on a private conversation. The cord was so long and the hall so short, you could take the telephone into the parlor, the bedroom, or the kitchen, where Mrs. Farisee had it now.

Aida didn't even try to talk first. She stood listening to me. Leaving the string beans she was fixing in the colander, Mrs. Farisee went to fetch Antony.

"You heard about the ants and Antony's hand?" I asked my father.

"Oh, yes."

"He has company."

"Antony?"

62

"Some kid about his age. Must be from school."

"Great! How are they getting along?"

"Fine."

"How's everything else?"

I looked at my sister, who was sitting on a kitchen chair looking out the window. "Okay."

I didn't ask him whether Mrs. Farisee had told him about my hair. I couldn't bear to bring it up. It wasn't likely that she had—a son's frozen scalded hand was enough for a father to hear about long distance. I didn't mention seeing Shirley, either, since there was no point getting into the matter of my taking a ride without permission. "How's the convention?"

"Not bad. Is Mrs. Farisee still taking you all to the museum tonight?"

"Unless it would be better for Antony to stay home." *Please, please,* I thought, *let Mrs. Farisee decide we will all stay home.*

I handed the telephone to Aida next, but she didn't say much.

Mrs. Farisee returned with Antony and Preston.

"Oh, wow." Preston stared at my head.

Antony, too, was so struck by my haircut that he kept his eyes on me, while muttering only an occasional "yes" and "no" and "okay" to my father.

"For this, the man made a long distance call?" Mrs. Farisee demanded, when my brother hung up.

His gaze remained fixed on my hair. "Dad wants to know if you're taking us to see the paintings tonight," he told Mrs. Farisee.

She sat down heavily. "I have had glass smashed in my sink, ants loosed in my kitchen, and a morning at the hospital with a frozen parboiled child. As soon as dinner is over, I am going to my room and putting my feet up. I would not leave this house to meet Vincent van Gogh in person."

Though I was preoccupied with my hair, I could see how seriously frazzled Mrs. Farisee was. She had never before given any hint that she was not totally in charge of her world.

"That means you're not taking us?" Antony asked.

My relief was mixed with regret. I'd been looking forward to the van Gogh exhibit. Since its world tour started, magazines and newspapers and radio and television had promoted it. They had convinced me I needed to go; that if I didn't, I would still be regretting the loss at sixty.

The twins had taken no interest in van Gogh until they'd seen a television program which brought up his cutting off his ear. Since then, they'd been fascinated by him.

Reading Mrs. Farisee's narrowed gaze as a confirmed refusal, Antony began negotiating. "How about we go on a bus with Dez? She's almost thirteen."

Mrs. Farisee did not bargain. "Twelve and a half, and she's not taking you twenty miles to a big city and back on a bus at night."

"They could come with us," Preston volunteered.

"My mom's taking my brother and me. She tried to make my father come, but he says he'll be bringing work home from the office. My brother tried to get out of it, too, but my mother won't let him. She told him a chance like this comes once in a lifetime, and when he grows up he'll never forgive her if she lets him pass it by. I'd kind of like to have somebody with us that wants to be there."

"You'll have your mother," Mrs. Farisee reminded him.

"She'll be working in the gift shop. She's a decent."

"You mean a docent," Mrs. Farisee told him.

"Yeah. She said being a museum decent is like being on the symphony guild—it's the way you meet all the people who count. She says that's how you get anywhere, by knowing the people who count. She didn't know she'd have to put in her volunteer time working in the gift shop before she gets to show visitors through the museum and give lectures and stuff." He turned to Antony. "So you guys want to come with us?"

"Mmm." Mrs. Farisee was noncommittal. "You'd have to keep a close eye on the twins, Desdemona."

"I'd just as soon stay home," I told her.

"Then you're not going," Mrs. Farisee told the twins.

"But Preston's mother will take us!" Antony protested.

Mrs. Farisee was unmoved. "If she wants to let

her sons run around a museum unsupervised, that's her business. You two are not going to wander through any exhibit without somebody tending you."

"There'll be such a crowd they're planning to let people through in batches," I ventured. "That means there'll be dozens of decents . . ."

"Docents. They're not going to let volunteer docents handle crowds at an exhibition like this. There'll also be guards. Docents and guards are not there to baby-sit and the subject is closed."

Antony and Aida and Preston looked at me as if I'd banned Christmas. Nobody can gaze at you as bleakly as a five-year-old who feels betrayed.

A horn sounded outside.

"Excuse me." Preston went to the parlor. He was back in a minute. "It's my mother," he told Antony. "I'll ask her, and you get your sister to change her mind."

As Antony took him to get his coat, I heard Preston ask, "Didn't your parents *murder* her for getting her hair all cut off?"

My brother came straight back to the kitchen after he walked Preston to the door. He had to hang around to be sure I knew that he was ignoring me.

Aida sat in the kitchen chair, ignoring all of us.

"Hey, wait a minute." I was indignant. "You guys pour Varathane in the shampoo bottle and make me lose my hair. You scald and freeze your stupid hand and break your ant farm and I'm the one who has to be seen nearly bald with a dumb kid and a

66

wagon full of ants. Now you're mad because I won't take you to a museum?"

Wordlessly, Antony trudged toward our bedroom. Aida headed for the parlor.

"If you charge after them," Mrs. Farisee warned me, "a boot-camp haircut will be the least of your troubles."

I sat down, seething. "They're a whole different generation, do you know that?"

"Every five years is a new generation lately," she observed.

"When I was their age, the Three Stooges gave me nightmares. These kids grow up with preview clips from slasher films flashed at them in the middle of almost every television program. Their idea of a film classic is the original *Night of the Living Dead*. They don't care about van Gogh's art. They care about his ear."

"Put the telephone back and stay away from the twins."

Looping the cord as I walked, I carried the telephone to the rickety hall table, then came back to watch Mrs. Farisee.

With Aida in the parlor and Antony in our room, the only place in the house to avoid them was in the kitchen. If I tried to take refuge in the bathroom, somebody was sure to have to use it.

Mrs. Farisee carried the colander to the kitchen table, put it on a dish towel, and began cracking the string beans. Anybody seeing the cool, decisive precision with which she snapped them would know that she should have been running an army, or at least a corporation. As I sat down across from her, she moved the colander closer to me. "Make yourself useful."

We had cracked most of the beans when Aida wandered into the kitchen. Edging closer to me, she slipped her hand in mine for a second. Then she headed for our bedroom.

"Don't try to forgive me," I yelled after her.

She and my brother came to dinner clean, without even being reminded.

The day had taken a lot out of us all. We ate quietly. Mrs. Farisee was past middle age, and she'd have us on her hands for a weekend that had begun in turmoil and wasn't over yet.

I was thinking about what I would do when Monday morning came.

Antony concentrated on eating, trying to manage with his left hand, using his fork very carefully and having a lot of trouble. His right hand, in a nest of bandages, rested on his lap.

Aida was quiet, too.

You know how a realization opens up for you with no warning. It's not out of the blue, it *is* the blue—a light bright blue that appears, expanding, expanding.

It hit me like that. Suddenly I knew how Aida was feeling. When she was separated from Antony at school, it must have seemed to her that she was losing part of her world. This day, she'd lost him while he was at home with her.

I put down my fork. "Okay. I suppose nobody my age is going to be allowed to go to the city alone at night. Nobody my age is going to risk being seen in public after sundown with a parent, for sure. And nobody, *nobody* from the high school is going to a museum on a Saturday night. How often do I get a chance to herd four little kids through an art exhibit all by myself? I mean, how lucky can I get?"

Five-year-olds do not understand sarcasm or sacrifice, but they were thrilled. The minute we finished dinner, Antony managed to dial Preston's number with his left hand. Having a friend meant even more to my brother than I'd realized. He had the number memorized.

Mrs. Farisee went into the hall to verify with Preston's mother that we were welcome. Then she sent the twins to change clothes while she and I did the dishes.

When we finished, I went to get ready for the museum. The twins were already dressed to go and in the parlor waiting.

Mrs. Farisee's laws were clear and firm. I knew she'd never let me wear slacks to a museum. Even if I wore boots, I'd have to wear knee socks or heavy tights.

I settled for a plaid skirt and pullover sweater with a pair of tan knee socks. I knew that, even if I could bring myself to wear her green-and-orange paisley kerchief, Mrs. Farisee would say it was not warm enough for evening. I tried tying my knit muffler around my skull, but no matter how I arranged it, it left the back of my head bare. Even if I'd had a hooded coat, I would look strange and sinister walking through the exhibit with the hood up. I would certainly be inviting more comments from Preston.

I told myself to think of the evening as a test, to harden me for the ordeal of school.

I went into the parlor. My brother was sitting near the front door. My sister sat on the other side of the room.

"Hey, Antony," I said. "You know your navy blue watch cap?"

"Watch cap?"

"You know. The dark blue knit hat Dad bought you at the surplus store. Do you mind if I wear it?"

He gazed at my hair. "You'd better wear it."

I found the cap where I'd tossed it when I was ransacking the toy box. I pulled the cap down over my ears and looked in the mirror, and was ready to back out of the trip. Then I told myself again sternly that escorting four little kids in a crowd of adults was only a way of working up to the time when I'd have to face my peers. I put on my coat and my rain boots and returned to the parlor just as the front bell rang.

I opened the door myself.

Preston stood on the porch.

Preston was not alone.

"This is my brother Mike," he said.

Mike Harbinger nodded, barely glancing at me.

I started to step back, but Mrs. Farisee and the twins were behind me.

"Don't you let them out of your sight," she cautioned as they squeezed past me, "and keep your hat pulled down over your ears so you don't catch your death. Even a sled dog clipped as close as you are would get chilled."

And I had thought the most harrowing test I had to face was school.

five

Seeing Mike Harbinger on my doorstep was so shattering, it paralyzed any instinct to flee. Silently, I followed the twins and the Harbinger brothers.

There I was, living the fantasy of every girl in my school, walking to a car with Mike Harbinger on a Saturday night.

No one in my class could be warped enough to imagine the fiendish twists given this reality—a Navy surplus watchcap over my stubbled head, three moppets scrambling into the back with me, and a woman in the front seat with an overweight basset hound beside her.

"This must be Anthony and his sisters," she greeted us. "I hope you don't mind if I let Michael drive. He just got his learner's permit, and his father and I want him to have as much practice as possible under our supervision before he's old enough to think about getting his license."

Mrs. Harbinger had the voice of one who has always been sure of her place in life, sure that place is near the top. Her tones were musical, her consonants were crisp, and she didn't bother to wait for answers.

"Check all the mirrors before you pull out," she instructed Mike, then turned her conversation back to the twins and me. "Even though the weather's cleared, I thought it was a good idea to leave early, since, of course, we don't allow Michael to drive on the highways. Actually, I wouldn't let him drive at all after daylight, but we'll take the back roads, and there won't be much traffic. Our town is fair-sized, but I'm afraid it's hardly a cultural mecca. I would imagine most of the crowds at the exhibit will be from the city itself."

Mike drove very slowly, very carefully, under a steady stream of warnings, exhortations, and advice from his mother.

"I hope you don't mind our bringing Wendell," Mrs. Harbinger said, turning her head slightly toward us again.

I wondered if we had yet to pick up Mr. Harbinger.

"If we leave him outside at night," she went on, "he howls so the neighbors complain, and if we keep him shut up inside, he has problems."

"He pees all over the house," Preston confided.

I decided Wendell had to be the dog.

"Preston," Mrs. Harbinger warned. "Wendell's

73

an old dog," she explained, "and he has a little diffi-culty with his bladder control."

"He can't hold it for more than—"

"Preston." Under those modulated tones lurked the steel of a Mrs. Farisee.

I felt an obligation to say something, since nei-ther the twins nor I had uttered a sound since we got in the car. I might look like a waterfront dere-lict, I might be out on a Saturday night with my brother and sister, but I didn't want Mike Harbin-ger thinking I was surly to boot. "Uh . . . have you thought of a dog door?" It seemed like a courteous and sensible suggestion.

"We have one, but we keep it locked when we're not home," Mrs. Harbinger said.

"Or else the neighbor's cat gets in and beats up Wendell," Preston added.

Mike Harbinger drove on, silent.

I suppose it takes a long time to recognize some-thing that goes counter to all you expect. It takes even longer when you're preoccupied by your own problems. Very gradually, it occurred to me that Mike Harbinger, who seemed to have had every gift, every advantage, lavished on him, was, right now, a miserably embarrassed fifteen-year-old boy. He was probably feeling so wretched he didn't even suspect how I was suffering.

He probably didn't even notice that I was a girl.

His mother supervised his driving meticulously and unrelentingly. She made him drive through the back streets of the city, and finally she said, "We'll park in that lot up ahead, Michael."

"It's another dozen blocks to the museum, Mom." That was not the voice of a star. This was the voice of everybody who has ever tried to reason with an implacable parent.

"I know what I'm doing, Michael. The lot is supervised, it is well lighted, and I am not going to park with you children on a city street at night. Besides, we'll never find a space any closer."

As the woman at the entrance booth gave Mike a ticket, Mrs. Harbinger leaned toward her. "Will you be good enough to keep an eye on our car? We'll have our basset locked in it."

"Basket?"

"Basset. Basset hound."

"I'm sorry. We can't be responsible for personal property."

Mrs. Harbinger was not ruffled. "He is not property. He is a purebred, registered basset hound." She fished in her purse, and handed Mike a bill. "Give her this, Michael."

I think the parking attendant was overwhelmed, realizing, as I did, that arguing with Mrs. Harbinger was like fighting marshmallow cream. Mike's mother would simply engulf any disagreement in a soft, relentless flow of words.

The attendant took the bill.

"Thank you so much. Go ahead, Michael," Mrs. Harbinger directed.

She told him which space to take, and had him back up twice to ease the car in at the angle she preferred. As she lifted Wendell out, she said, "Be sure you lock all the doors, Michael. And for goodness' sake, don't forget to take the keys. You remember how upset your father was when you locked us all out of the car."

She led Wendell and the rest of us from the parking lot, then handed the end of the leash to Mike. "Take him out to the curb, dear, and be sure he relieves himself."

Wendell plodded after Mike to the curb. The dog's attitude was much like Mike's, weary and resigned. As Wendell lifted his leg, Mike looked off down the street and I gazed the other way.

"There. Put him back in the car, Michael. Don't forget to lock it and leave the window down an inch or two for ventilation."

"I don't think we should leave him," Mike said.

"He'll be perfectly all right for a couple of hours," Mrs. Harbinger replied.

Mike was plainly uncomfortable arguing with her, but he didn't move. "He's old, and it's a cold night."

Preston took up the cause. "Somebody might steal him. The woman can't see him from where she is."

Mrs. Harbinger looked down at her younger son with barely perceptible impatience. "Who is going to steal an ancient basset hound with a bladder condition?"

"You just said he was a purebred registered." While Preston was clearly not happy disagreeing with his mother, neither was he daunted.

"And there are all the fumes from other cars," Mike added. "He already wheezes in his sleep."

"Oh, for heaven's sake!" Mrs. Harbinger snapped. "Bring him, then. I'll just have to keep him in the back of the gift shop and hope nobody makes a fuss." Taking Preston's hand, she strode toward the corner so fast he had to run.

We made an interesting group. Antony trotted beside Preston, pretending, out of natural courtesy, not to notice that Mrs. Harbinger was holding on to her son's hand in public.

Aida walked next to me. I'd never before known her to lag behind her brother.

To my astonishment, Mike fell into step beside us, the dog pottering along behind him. Who would have suspected that this teenage stunner not only stood up for dogs, but didn't scorn strangely dressed twelve-year-old humans? However this night might scar me, I would always remember that Mike Harbinger walked beside me of his own free will.

He didn't speak, of course. He was being dragged to a museum on a Saturday night with his mother, his little brother, a preteener in rain boots and a watch cap, and five-year-old twins, one heavily bandaged and the other heavily depressed.

I suppose, when you're miserable, you're better off not having to endure the company of a jolly, carefree group.

Mrs. Harbinger, however, was not one to let people suffer in peace. She glanced back at Mike. "You see? I was right about the parking. It's barely seven-twenty, and we haven't spotted a single empty space, and all the lots are filled. So," she addressed us all, "how much do we know about Vincent van Gogh?"

Aida looked up at me. Preston looked at the sidewalk. Only a wimp, I knew, would let herself be bullied into reciting everything she knew about van Gogh just to please Mrs. Harbinger. On the other hand, I didn't want to be rude, so I tried to look sincerely interested.

Keeping her grip on Preston, relying upon him not to guide her into the gutter, she looked at Mike and me. "Vincent was born where?"

Never underestimate the power of marshmallow cream. I could not walk on silently when she asked a direct question. "The Netherlands."

"Yes!" In the next few blocks she filled us in on van Gogh's life and a brief history of Postimpressionist painting, without mentioning the severed ear. Nor did she bring up Vincent's onetime friend, Gauguin, who left wife and children and ran off to Tahiti to find himself.

There were hundreds of people in queue for the museum.

"Come along," Mrs. Harbinger told us. "Docents don't wait in line."

The people ahead of us turned to regard her with long, flinty stares.

"Mom, we're not docents." Mike's voice was low. "Everybody else has been standing here. . . ."

"There's no point waiting out here in the cold," Mrs. Harbinger told him.

"I'd rather," he said.

She turned to me.

"I don't mind waiting." While the idea of remaining on display was disheartening, the worst had already happened. Mike had seen me. I didn't have the nerve to sweep past all the people in line. Also, I wasn't convinced that even a docent could whisk us in ahead of them without causing, at the very least, a barrage of hostile comments.

"All right. All right. Then I will just have to freeze out here with you."

"Mom, you don't have to," Mike told her, almost pleading.

"Dear," she said gently, "I am responsible for you all. How would I feel if the twins' mother just turned Preston over to Dorothea at night in the city?"

No self-respecting person can consent to be drowned in marshmallow. "I think the two of us can look after the three of them," I said. "We'll be very careful."

Mike Harbinger might have to endure being seen with a twelve-year-old in a stocking cap. Once he got home, he would probably forget I existed. But at least I was not going to earn his disrespect.

His mother hesitated a moment. "Very well. I will leave you here, then. I'll ask the guards to keep an

79

eye on you, and I want you all to behave. Michael, you and Dorothea must stay right together and hold the little ones by the hand at all times. If anybody has to go to the bathroom, be sure you all go together so you don't get separated."

"Ma!" Preston looked scandalized.

"No, no, no, dear," his mother assured him. "If you or Anthony have to go, Michael will take you both in and Dorothea will wait outside with her sister. And if her sister has to go . . ."

"I know," Aida said politely.

"As soon as the tour is over, you all come directly to the museum gift shop. You may look at things, but you're to handle them carefully and behave like ladies and gentlemen until my shift there ends. Do you understand?"

Preston and Mike nodded.

"Dorothea?"

"Desdemona," I said. "I understand."

After Antony and Aida promised her that they, too, understood, she left us.

Immediately, Preston began talking, as if he had to release all the conversation he'd held in for an hour. Since he talked only to Antony, Aida and Mike and I were left to shuffle in silence toward the head of the line.

Regardless of my father's theories, I could imagine Mike Harbinger being interviewed in fifteen or twenty years. The reporter would ask him about the worst time in his life, and Mike would say, "One Saturday night when I was fifteen, my mother made me take a bunch of kids to a museum." I glanced at him quickly. He was looking straight ahead, stoic. Besides everything else, he had a great profile. *No,* I decided. *No. Dreadful as this evening is, Mike Harbinger has so much going on in his life that, in a year, he'll barely remember it.*

So we edged ahead, Mike herding Preston, Preston talking steadily to Antony, Aida holding my hand. There we were, Mike and Aida and I, with hundreds of people packed around us, each of us totally alone.

It took half an hour of alternately standing still and shuffling forward before we got to the head of the line. Then, for another half hour, we were processed through a maze of red velvet ropes, as if we'd come to the post office during the holiday mailing rush. Once we got into the first room of the van Gogh exhibit, we were left to move on at our own speed.

Mike kept a hand on his brother's shoulder, and Antony stuck close to Preston, so I followed right behind them with Aida.

One Christmas when we lived in California and the twins were just babies, my mother took me to see *The Nutcracker* at the San Francisco Opera House. There were just the two of us, my mother driving, both of us all dressed up, just the two of us together.

I remember looking out the car windows at the traffic in the other lanes, feeling proud that my mother was such a good driver. She wore her good black coat. Her hair was soft and blonde, and in profile she looked like a cameo. I had a red coat with a velveteen collar and new black patent leather shoes. The most important thing was that there were just the two of us.

The Opera House was full, mostly women and the kids they'd brought, all dressed up, to see *The Nutcracker.*

I can even remember how the audience smelled—a blending of bath powder and faint perfumes. At zoos and amusement parks the smell is a hodgepodge of sweat and caramel corn and stale wet diapers. At the Opera House the scents, like the voices, the lights, the colors, the textures of the clothes, were rich and formal, and so exciting it made me dizzy.

We sat in the first balcony, while people found their seats and looked through their programs. It was one of those times that is set so perfectly in your memory that you can bring it all back, the colors, sounds, smells, as if it were still happening.

It was the first ballet I'd ever been to, and with all that *setting,* I knew it was going to be wonderful. In the first minutes, when everything on the stage was a surprise, it was. Then I tried too hard to concentrate on the ballet, so I wouldn't miss anything, so I'd have it all to take home, and probably because I knew I was supposed to appreciate it. I tried so hard my attention cracked, and then wandered, and then I felt guilty.

It was different now, at the van Gogh exhibit. I

was not with my mother. I did not have the certainty that I looked right, and therefore belonged. I was mortified by how wrong I looked. I had layer upon layer of worries.

With so much on my mind, I couldn't concentrate, so I just looked at the paintings. After a while I forgot about the crowd, and how I looked, and how Mike was feeling. There were only the paintings, and the stillness inside when you confront something that's so good it astonishes you.

I started to lift Aida so she could see better, but she twitched away like a cat that doesn't want to be carried. We moved on in a crush of people.

"Hey, wow!" Preston said to Antony. "Look at those stars! I bet that's just how stars look if you're nearsighted."

And Aida made her move.

From her pocket, she took the bag of carob chips she'd bought that morning, and held them out to Preston. "Want some?"

It was so fine, the kind of gesture that probably helped lift our whole species from savagery. Instead of cherishing her hurt, or being rotten, she held out that bag to the enemy.

And I had to slap down her great gesture. There were signs all over forbidding food and drink. "Aida, you're not allowed . . ."

"Eeeyeww!" Preston drew back. *"Ants!"*

Besides its phenomenal staying power, Preston's voice carried.

As people followed his gaze, the polite murmuring that had surrounded us was rippled by muted exclamations of dismay. All we needed was Bramwell Grove to stir up the crowd with reminders of Charlton Heston and the army ants.

I couldn't hustle Aida to a bathroom. There was no hurrying through a crush like this, and I certainly didn't want to shove my sister and her bag of ant-covered carob chips at people who were already edgy. Besides, tossing ants in the bathroom's trash container would certainly get them killed.

I took the knit glove off my left hand, snatched the bag from Aida, and stuffed it into the glove.

The people who had been nearest us moved ahead as quickly as they could.

Though I was tempted to shake off the ants crawling up my fingers, I picked them off carefully, flicked them gently into the glove, and held the wrist closed, knowing the occupants would be finding their way out before long.

Mike Harbinger watched me as if he were witnessing a bizarre but fascinating ritual.

I forced myself to speak directly to him. "You wouldn't have a rubber band or anything?"

He shook his head. "Maybe we'd better go."

People who had been behind us were edging around us, cautiously.

"Not before we see the picture where his ear's cut off," Antony protested.

"*Ear's cut off?*" Preston's voice again drew the attention of everyone around us.

Being far below adult eye level, and concerned with something irresistibly gruesome, Preston had no idea of the effect he was creating. *"Ear's cut off? Whose?"*

"Van Gogh's, and shut up," Mike told him.

Preston was too shocked and excited to worry about keeping his voice down. "Somebody cut off *van Gogh's* ear? Who?"

"Van Gogh," Mike said, trying to move him through the crowd.

There is no way to budge a kid who is consumed by an urgent need to know something. *"I mean, who cut off his ear?"*

"Van Gogh cut off van Gogh's ear." Mike got a firmer grip on his brother.

"HE CUT OFF HIS OWN EAR? THAT'S WORSE THAN FREEZING OFF YOUR HAND!" Preston cried.

Antony gazed at his bandaged arm. *"Freeze it off?"*

"That's enough!" As I reached for my brother, I dropped the ant-filled glove.

"My ants!"

Aida dived for the glove.

Hauling her up, I grabbed Antony and dragged them past years of van Gogh's work.

Luckily, this was a museum crowd, made up, except for us, of people with respect for culture and civilization. Even their annoyance was restrained as we squirmed and struggled toward the green EXIT sign.

As I reached it, two guards flanking the door stepped forward. "I'm sorry," one told me. "Would you mind going . . ."

"We've got a glove full of ants here." Mike Harbinger, behind me, put his hand on my shoulder.

He actually put his hand on my shoulder. Mike Harbinger did.

". . . Ants?"

"A swarm," Mike assured the guard.

The second guard opened the door. "Don't try coming back," he said as I ushered the twins through.

I strode across the pavement, so paranoid I didn't dare run for fear it might look as if I'd used the ants to cover our theft of a van Gogh.

The minute I reached the bushes, I grabbed the glove from my sister.

Holding it by one finger, I shook out the bag so the ants wouldn't be trapped. I tucked glove and bag under a cotoneaster, then blew a few ants off my fingers.

Preston, with Mike and the twins, stood watching.

"You're littering," he said.

I reminded myself that, however he resembled his mother, he was only five years old, and short at that. "Preston—Preston, there is nothing else to do with a glove full of ants and candy. Have you ever tried to get ants out of a knit glove, Preston? You want me to carry that glove around the streets *all night* looking for a trash can? You want those ants, who have lived up to now in an ant farm, to be dumped in a trash can and picked up and *crushed* in a trash masher? You want me to bring them in your mother's car?"

Preston did not abash easily. "If my mother finds out we're wandering around here at night, she'll have a cow. And, boy, when she finds out you just about started a riot in there. . . ."

"*I* started a riot? If you hadn't started yelling about cut-off ears and hands, Preston—"

Mike drew his brother back from my wrath. "We'd better go around front and wait for my mom."

"Yeah," Preston told me. "Before you're picked up for disturbing the peace."

While standing by the side exit of a museum at night yelling at a five-year-old was no crime, I couldn't be sure that somebody we'd offended inside hadn't complained.

We walked around to the front of the building.

"I don't think we'd better try to go in again," I told Mike.

"I would not take any of these three in there again for anything," he said flatly.

I was still apprehensive. "Do you think we look suspicious hanging around outside here?"

"Act casual," Preston advised.

"I'd better go in and tell my mother where we are," Mike decided.

"She said we were absolutely to stick together," Preston reminded him.

I had to agree with this kid who could have turned Mother Teresa against the human race. "She did. And she was . . . very firm."

"I guess she'll know we're out here." Mike stood with one foot on the sidewalk, one on the lowest step, his back against a pedestal with a copy of Rodin's *The Thinker* on it. Just *standing*, Mike Harbinger was a study in how to look terrific.

And I realized that I hadn't thought about how he looked or who he was for . . . well, close to half an hour. What he had been, all along, was a person you'd want around in an emergency.

He cleared his throat. "So . . . how did the ants get from the farm into your sister's coat pocket?"

I told him about that morning, about the ant farm and Antony's burned hand and relocating the ants. The story was harrowing, even now. Still, I did not mention my hair. Even when your audience is enthralled, you do not call attention to the fact that you are almost bald.

"What are you doing out here?" Mrs. Harbinger came hurrying down the museum steps. Her voice could have shattered a museum chandelier. "I told you you were to come directly to the gift shop!"

"We . . . had to leave," Mike said.

"That's no excuse! You deliberately disobeyed me, every one of you, and I could have been worried *sick!*"

"I'm sorry." Mike sounded sincere, but not intimidated. "I didn't think you'd want us all hanging around in there too long."

"You didn't think! You didn't think at all. I am furious, Michael!"

I could hardly stand by and let him take the blame. "Actually, it was my—"

"I don't want to hear another word about it! I even had to leave the dog back in there."

"Do you want me to go get him?" Mike asked.

"I do not want any one of you moving one inch from this spot until I come back. Not an inch!" Mrs. Harbinger walked around to the side of the museum, her high heels punishing the pavement.

None of us spoke.

There are few things more embarrassing than being with somebody whose mother has just jumped all over him. You're too ashamed to say anything until enough time has passed that you can act as if it never happened and change the subject. Despite my discomfort, I was aware that Mike Harbinger, besides being gorgeous, athletic, smart, and nice, had more class than anybody I knew, except my father. I didn't deepen his humiliation, of course, by saying anything about his taking the blame for us all.

Even Preston showed some sense by keeping quiet.

Of course, Mrs. Harbinger hadn't berated him. We didn't know one another well enough, or have the presence of mind, to dredge up a change of subject. The longer the silence went on, the more strained it would have seemed to say anything to break it. Instead, we stood around, trying to look

89

interested in the museum architecture, or absorbed in private thoughts.

Mrs. Harbinger returned, leading Wendell. By then she'd gone from indignation to silent disapproval. We all walked back to the car without talking, standing mute each time Wendell stopped to wet a bush or a street sign.

At the car, Mike unlocked the door on his mother's side first and lifted Wendell in.

On the way home, Mrs. Harbinger broke the silence. As before, she coached Mike's driving: warning, advising, correcting, but in a low, flat, cold voice. She didn't ask how we liked the exhibit, or try to tell us more about van Gogh.

Aida fell asleep, leaning against me. When she started to snore, I let her. Mike and his mother couldn't think any worse of us.

When we stopped at our house, I nudged my sister awake and said "Thank you" to Mrs. Harbinger. Prompted by her, Mike got out and opened the car door and walked the twins and me to the porch.

"Thanks," I said.

He nodded. " 'Night."

Mrs. Farisee was in the parlor reading a paperback, which she tucked into the pocket of her robe as we entered. "Did you have a nice time?"

"If I had a diary," I told her, "I'd burn it."

six

Sherman didn't come over until long after church on Sunday. He came to the back door, as usual.

"I was beginning to think you'd decided to stick around your own home long enough to get acquainted with it," Mrs. Farisee greeted him, then took the newspaper back to her room.

"I had to get out of there," he told me. "They made me straighten my whole room and wash Jake, and they're still in a cleaning frenzy."

"On a Sunday?" I wondered whether Mrs. Farisee had taken the television section with her.

"It's the party."

"What party?" I was glad to see she'd left the comics section on the kitchen table.

"My parents' big party to announce my dad's running for mayor. I told you." He didn't seem aggrieved that I'd forgotten. I suppose it happened to him often. "They had to invite all the important

91

people who'd be insulted if he didn't tell them he was running for mayor before he announces that he is."

"You mean they don't know it? Everybody says your father is going to run for mayor. It's in the paper all the time."

"Sure, everybody knows, but he hasn't *announced* it. He has to tell all the important people at one time so they won't get mad because he told somebody else first. He has to tell them, and then Monday he's holding a press conference to announce it. And, boy—are my parents tense! Our maid quit yesterday because my mother was driving her crazy, and then we couldn't find a cleaning service to come in at the last minute."

"Your house is always clean. Your house is immaculate."

"Listen, before a party they even have the windowsills waxed. I think they're afraid somebody will sneak a look into my room or get a whiff of the dog bed and decide we're not perfect. Of course, they're extra stressed because they have to invite my uncle Bramwell. He kind of undermines the way they want people to see us. He's like unwaxed sills or clutter under the bed."

"Why don't they present him like a diamond in the rough?"

"My uncle," Sherman said flatly, "is a mine field in the rough. They don't dare not invite him—he's got more money than they'll ever have. Besides, if he didn't come, everybody would be wondering why."

"Doesn't anybody like him?"

Sherman was thoughtful. "You know, in a way I almost do. He drives my parents crazy."

Mrs. Farisee refused to let Sherman come with us to pick up my father. "I am paid to look after three children, not to cart their friends everywhere I go."

I dreaded taking my head out in public again, but she wouldn't let me stay home. "I do not plan to return and find that somebody has put motor oil in the mayonnaise jar, and I am not taking two five-year-olds without you to help keep them quiet."

At the airport, Mrs. Farisee told me I could not wait in the car.

"I'll keep the windows up and the doors locked," I promised.

"Come."

Walking through the airport, I kept the watch cap pulled way over my ears.

The minute Antony and Aida spotted our father, they were all over him. Immediately, Aida started telling him about Antony's hand, and the ants. She did not mention my hair or my haircut, the ride with Bramwell, or the trip to the museum.

With all Aida's breathless talking, my father didn't have a chance to ask me why I was looking like a merchant seaman braving a sou'wester.

There must be an amnesia that affects us sometime in our teens. Little kids are a hundred times more observant, and more sensitive, than adults choose to recall. My sister was spilling over, recounting Antony's accident and the ant farm adventure in riveting detail. Probably without even trying, she edited out all the parts she and Antony and I wouldn't want our father to know.

When we got home, I kept the cap on, but nobody noticed.

My father had brought us all presents, even a clock radio for Mrs. Farisee. I could see she was pleased. She had an alarm clock and her own radio and television set, but it was nice that he thought of her as someone who might like waking to music.

The minute we'd unwrapped our gifts, Antony asked, "Can Preston come over?"

"*May* Preston come over," my father said automatically. There's a certain security in little things like that. A parent who has never yet gotten his kid to say *may* instead of *can* never stops trying. "Who's Preston?"

"My friend."

"Oh! Sure. So long as I don't have to pick him up." As soon as Antony went to telephone Preston, my father asked me, "What's this friend like?"

"I am not in a position to give an unbiased opinion."

"He is a perfect little gentleman," Mrs. Farisee said, "and you may not wear that stocking cap all day and all night in the house, Desdemona." She left the room.

I didn't wait for my father to ask questions. "Let me tell you about my hair before you see it, and please don't say anything when you do see it, because if you do I know I'll cry."

Being a psychologist, of course, he was good at listening. He sat quietly, giving me all his attention, while I explained about the varnish and the Mona Lisa. Before I knew it, I was telling about Mike Harbinger and everything that happened at the museum, and finally about Bramwell and Shirley and the dog.

When I finished, he shook his head and muttered "Oh, boy," as if he understood just how it had been and just how I felt. I was sure that if I asked him in a week, he could repeat everything I'd told him without missing anything important.

Finally, I took off the cap. My father looked at my hair solemnly. I was glad he didn't try to tell me it looked okay, or remind me that it would grow out.

The telephone rang, which was just as well. I'd been telling him my problems without even giving him a chance to call Shirley.

Mrs. Farisee opened the door from the hall. "Sherman's on the line, Desdemona."

Sherman sounded ill at ease. "My mother made me call," he told me. "She wants to borrow you."

"*Borrow* me?"

"That's how she put it. She leaned so hard on the caterer's crew that they all walked out. The caterer is hanging in there by a thread. There's nobody to help him and to take coats and empty ashtrays, except me."

"Sherman, does she know how my hair looks?"

"Right now my parents would accept you if you'd tattooed your skull. They'll just keep you in the kitchen."

When I hesitated, he went on. "Look, I don't want to tell you what to do. But if I were renting a house from them and had three dogs and no lease and no place else to go, I think I'd . . ."

"I know."

"On the one hand, it's blackmail. On the other hand, I'm thinking of you and the dogs out in the cold even before the condo deal."

"Tell her yes."

"Good. I didn't want to push you, Dez, but I need a friend here, too."

"What do I wear?"

"A dress, but nothing so fancy you look like company."

"When?"

"Soon as you can. The party starts at four."

Though I dreaded taking my head out, even to the Groves' kitchen, I knew Sherman was right.

I went back to my father. "Sherman's parents are stuck. They're having a big party, and everybody but the caterer has walked out on them. They asked if I could come help."

"You want to?"

"Sure." I couldn't let him know I was doing it because I didn't dare risk the Groves' ill will. Should he have to face the knowledge that his daughter was going to work in the landlord's kitchen to delay her family's being thrown out on the streets?

Mrs. Farisee made me eat before I left. She knew what she was doing. Sherman's parents would never have invited me or anybody in my family as a guest. At least I wouldn't get hungry while I was there. If they offered me food, I could honestly say, "No, thanks. I've eaten."

I owned three winter dresses. Since the Groves would keep me in the kitchen, I chose the coolest one.

Mrs. Farisee came into the bedroom with the scarf she'd worn to church. It was either silk or a good imitation. "This is a little more respectable," she said. "Try tying it with the knot behind your head. It might look more dressy."

My father drove me to the Groves'.

"I hope they won't want me to take the scarf off in the house," I said.

"Did I ever tell you about my stepfather's aunt?"

"I don't know." I could not have been less interested in stories about his relatives. In my mind, I was rehearsing what I would say if Mrs. Grove told me to take the scarf off my head. I could say I was coming down with something, which might very well be true, but then she might be annoyed with me for bringing germs into the house. I could say I thought it would be more sanitary if I'd be handling food. Then she might be offended that I took it upon myself to tell her what was sanitary.

My father talked on, ignoring my lack of attention. "I was eight or ten when I first met her. She must have been over sixty. Even at my age, I could tell she wore a wig. Either it wasn't a very good wig, or the fact that she had no eyebrows or eyelashes was the tip-off. She'd lost every hair, even on her arms and legs, when she was in her teens."

"How?" I was so startled I forgot my own train of thought.

"Scarlet fever, diphtheria—I'm not sure. Something kids don't get anymore. But her hair never grew back."

"This is supposed to cheer me up?"

He didn't smile, but he wasn't ruffled. "Do you want to strike a pose or admit that you'll have a decent head of hair in a few months?"

"This is supposed to make me feel shallow for taking a mere scalping so hard." I was not going to admit that I wanted to hear more about his step-father's aunt.

He went on as if I hadn't interrupted. "She never married. Besides being bald, she was nearly six feet tall, and this was generations ago, remember. She had a long face and great wonderful sad eyes like Virginia Woolf's, but unfortunately she did not have Virginia Woolf's elegant nose."

By this time, I was thoroughly engrossed. "Who's Virginia Woolf?"

"A writer. As a matter of fact, in the twenties and thirties she wrote about the need of women for independence and the freedom to be creative. Anyway, Serena, my stepfather's aunt, had a magnificent nose. It would have looked splendid on an aging Roman emperor. In profile, she resembled an eagle, and if you say bald eagle, you may walk the rest of the way to the Groves'."

"Go on." I was so wrapped up in Serena's story, I wasn't even indignant at the suggestion that I might joke about her.

"She was a recluse. I would guess that when she was young, her parents kept her tucked away to protect her, since she looked so dramatically different from what was considered to be acceptable for a woman." He stopped at an intersection, and, while his eyes were on the road, I realized he was seeing her somewhere in his mind.

Gazing at his profile, I noticed that his own hair was already thinning at the temples. He wasn't handsome like Harley or Bramwell Grove, but he was a very presentable man. He looked like a person who thought a lot, and worried, and was kind and decent, and I was glad he was my father. I was even glad he'd gone back to wearing his glasses; contact lenses reminded me of the phase after my mother left when he was dating women who looked like the extras in MTV videos.

"But you didn't meet this aunt until she was over sixty?" I asked, to remind him he was talking to me.

He nodded, and drove on. "I used to love visiting her. She was a cultured woman: brilliant, gentle, well read. Most of all, she had a generous heart, a generous spirit. Her instincts must have been fine to begin with, so her judgment was humane and original. When I was thirty, and she couldn't get around without a walker, I realized I'd been in love with her for years."

"In love?"

He nodded. "That, my child, is how our age has cheated you. I'm not talking about the kind of love that sells paperbacks and movie tickets. You can be in love without any kind of physical desire."

I could understand what he meant. On the other hand, I could see that writers or filmmakers who dealt with that kind of love were not likely to have enormous audiences. I wondered if any of them would ever dare present a heroine like Serena.

"It's a dirty trick," he said, "to convince the young that they're worthless unless they look like models, with bodies perfected by Nautilus machines, makeup hiding every flaw."

"If you meant to make me feel better, did you kind of wander off the subject?" I asked.

"No. I meandered through it."

A wide circular driveway led to the Groves' front door. Along the sides and back of the lot were towering Italian cypresses, almost trunk to trunk.

"Call me when you're ready to leave," my father said. "I'm going to swing by Shirley's. If I'm not home, I'll be there."

"I was wondering when you were going to get around to her."

"I called her while you were dressing, but first her line was busy and then there was no answer. She's probably back home by now."

He let me out and drove on.

As I walked up the driveway to the front entrance, I heard a car pull in and stop.

Mrs. Grove must have been waiting for any sign of help, because she answered the door herself. "Desdemona, thank heavens!" She was still in her robe. Sherman, beside her, wore a white shirt, dark trousers, and a necktie.

"Let me collect my thoughts, Desdemona." Mrs. Grove pressed delicate fingers to her temples. "It's going to be a matter of where we need you most." While she looked distraught, she was not disheveled. Her robe was a dark wine-colored velvet, and her high-heeled slippers were purple satin.

As the people from the car came up the steps, she stopped talking. Sherman stared past me in astonishment.

"Hey, Sherman. Dez." It was Shirley Miller's voice.

I turned.

Shirley Miller stood there with Mona and Lisa— and Bramwell Grove.

I tried to speak, but I could only nod. Sherman's "Oh. Hi," sounded as surprised as I felt.

Mrs. Grove recovered her voice, if not her manners. "It's a nightmare," she greeted Bramwell.

"The fireplace is belching, *belching* smoke and ash, and Harley is in there making it worse. The dog has taken a violent dislike to the caterer. The downstairs bathroom is backed up, which means, of course, that it's going to affect the rest of the house, and we can't get a plumber." Her glance kept straying to Mona and Lisa.

Mona wore a short, imitation leopard Orlon coat over her pink uniform. Lisa's coat was made of white fake fur. She and Mona gazed at Mrs. Grove stoically, like prisoners determined not to crack under interrogation.

"You know Shirley Miller," Bramwell said.

Sherman's mother managed to focus on Shirley and to smile without moving anything but her lips. "Shirley. What a pleasant surprise."

"And Mona and Lisa," Bramwell added.

Mrs. Grove really looked at them then—as if she were certain they'd come to the wrong house.

"They were good enough to come help you out of your mess," Bramwell prompted his sister-in-law.

Her face remained fixed in that smile. "How very kind. Sherman, take the ladies back to the maid's room and show them where to leave their wraps."

I smiled at Shirley, feeling sheepish that I'd even imagined she'd come with Bramwell socially. Nevertheless, I didn't trust the man's intentions. He stood too close to her, for one thing.

Since I wasn't sure whether I was included among the "ladies," I stood waiting for instructions from Mrs. Grove.

Mona and Lisa stepped into the foyer and followed Sherman down the hall. Shirley didn't.

Mrs. Grove kept smiling until Mona and Lisa were out of earshot. Then she asked Bramwell, her voice quiet but intense, "Who are they?"

"Mona and Lisa."

"I mean, who *are* they?"

"The only people I could put the arm on to work at your shindig on an hour's notice. And they have uniforms."

"*Pink nylon?* Pink nylon uniforms with white orthopedic wedgies?"

"They're hairdressers! What do you want? You want me to pop by the mortuary and see if any of their embalmers are free?"

A howl came from Bramwell's car.

"There. Now you've got my dog upset."

"Your dog! What dog?" Mrs. Grove demanded.

"Shirley found him, and now I'm stuck with him," Bramwell said. "He's ... attached to me. I can't go from one room to another without him at my heels. Smartest little guy you'd ever want to meet. Just this morning he—"

"I'd better reassure him." Shirley hurried off to the car.

"I don't appreciate you pulling your snob routine in front of my date," Bramwell told Mrs. Grove in a low voice. "I would like her to think this family has a little more class."

I had to stand there. I could not humiliate my father or myself by letting these people see how I felt.

Only a minute ago I had been ashamed of doubting Shirley!

Mrs. Grove glanced at me. "You go on back to the kitchen, Desdemona. The caterer can tell you what to do." Then she coughed. Behind her the foyer was beginning to look hazy, and I could smell the smoke.

Walking down the hall to the back of the house, I thought of my father, driving over to Shirley's apartment, maybe even waiting around for her.

Sherman was standing outside the maid's room, his back against the wall. "I don't think those women want to be here," he confided.

I knew I'd better not try to speak until I had my feelings under control. I went into the maid's room. Mona was peering in the mirror, wiping something off her tooth with her little finger.

I put my coat on the bed with the leopard Orlon and the white acrylic.

Lisa came out of the bathroom adjusting her bra straps. "Up and at 'em," she said bleakly.

"Hey," Mona reminded me as I started for the hall, "you still have your scarf on your head."

I couldn't tell them I was hiding their work. I took it off.

As I came out of the maid's room with Mona and Lisa, Sherman got his first look at my haircut. His eyes widened and his mouth opened, and then he collected himself. "Well. Um . . . Well. I guess we'd better go to the kitchen."

The Groves' kitchen was enormous. Under a window was a long stainless steel sink flanked by yards of tiled counters and wooden cabinets. Beside the six-burner range against a side wall were two ovens plus a microwave suspended under a cabinet. Even the refrigerator was oversized. In the center of the room was a work island, with dozens of fancy bowls and trays and platters on its butcher-block top. A three-tier serving cart stood next to the island.

The kitchen had three doors—the one we came through, a back door to the laundry room, and a swinging door that led into the dining room. A thread of smoke was wisping in around the swinging door.

A tall, heavy man in a dark suit and white apron stood at the sink. Despite the cold, the window in front of him was open.

On the counter at his left were stacks and stacks of tiny bread slices, ranging from pale cream color to dark, dark brown. Behind the bread were more than a dozen boxes of crackers, brands I'd never seen on a supermarket shelf. The counter on his right looked like a display of loot from a gourmet deli robbery—jars, cans, bottles, little crockery tubs, boxes of fancy toothpicks, an array of knives and openers.

"This is our caterer," Sherman told us.

Mona and Lisa looked around the kitchen, wary as zebras picking their way to a crocodile-infested water hole.

Sherman addressed the caterer's back. "These are Miss Mona and Miss Lisa, and Desdemona Blank."

The caterer turned. His gaze swept from Mona's and Lisa's hair over their shiny pink uniforms to their orthopedic shoes, and then from my shoes up to my hair. A muscle under his left eye twitched.

"He's running a few hours behind schedule," Sherman explained.

"What do you want us to do?" Mona asked.

"Peel the shrimp," the caterer said.

"Peel the shrimp," Mona repeated to Lisa, but her tone said, *Didn't I tell you?*

The door from the dining room swung open. Mrs. Grove, in stocking feet, wearing a shimmering blue dress that looked fragile as butterfly wings, swept in, along with a smoky haze. Moving the caterer aside, she bent to open the cupboard doors under the sink and stick her head in. After a moment, she backed out, yelling, "It isn't in there!"

From the parlor came Mr. Grove's strangled shout, "Try the garage!"

Rising, Sherman's mother tiptoed out the back door.

The caterer waved his hands, trying to dispel the smoke. He turned back to the sink and shut the cupboard doors with his knee.

Then he jerked his head toward a colander full of shrimp that stood in the sink. "You clean them and shell them and arrange them appealingly on a plat-

106

ter," he told Mona, as he began opening containers arrayed on the counter.

Mona stepped up to the sink, and I eased over until I was far to the caterer's right, with my back against a counter. It seemed like a good idea to stay out of the traffic lanes.

Mrs. Grove came in from the laundry room. Before she could block him, Jake scurried past her. With a growl like a rat's gargle, he began savaging the caterer's trouser leg. The man did not move. He had probably heard somewhere that you should never run from an attacking animal.

"For heaven's sake, feed the dog!" Mrs. Grove commanded Sherman distractedly. Then she noticed my hair. "Oh, my word!"

"Where is the blessed plunger?" Mr. Grove yelled.

"It has to be in one of the bathrooms!" Mrs. Grove shouted, as she rushed out the door to the maid's room.

Sherman pried Jake from the caterer's trouser leg and handed the writhing, snarling beast to me.

"Excuse me," Sherman said. "I need the dog food." Squeezing past the caterer, he climbed up on the counter. His heel hit a jar, and olives and juice cascaded over the tiles.

"That does it." The caterer tore off his apron, threw it on the floor and strode past me and out the back door.

Mrs. Grove came in the side door, looking harried. "I *know* we have a plunger. There has got to be one in this house." She spied the apron on the floor. "That is absolutely uncalled for. That is totally unsanitary." She snatched it up and tossed it over a food processor. "Tell the caterer he's going to have to get some food out before the guests come," she instructed Sherman.

"I think he . . . left," Sherman said.

"Left? What for? How could a man who calls himself a professional run out of anything at this hour?"

Sherman climbed down off the counter, avoiding jars and juice and olives. "I don't think he's coming back."

Rushing to the back door, Mrs. Grove yanked it open.

She screamed.

"I'm sorry! I didn't mean to scare you." Mike Harbinger stood in the doorway, wearing slacks and jacket.

I should not have been surprised. Why should I have been surprised?

It was not only inevitable, it was necessary. I had shared hours of shame and misery with Mike Harbinger the evening before, but he had not seen my uncovered head. What is fate for, if not to give you one last kick when you think it has tired of abusing you?

Mrs. Grove's scream had roused Jake's feral instincts. As he struggled to get free, Mike looked at him. "Hey, dog."

It was too late to run. Mike looked at my hair. He looked me in the eyes, then he looked back at my hair. It took him only an instant to master his astonishment. "Hi," he told me. Then he turned his gaze back to Mrs. Grove. "Nobody answered the front door. I'm Mike Harbinger. My mom sent me over early. She said you needed help."

To slink out of the kitchen, I would have to cross it, or squeeze past Mike, or enter the Groves' dining room where I might see Shirley and Bramwell. There was no point, anyway. Mike had seen my hair. If I tried to slip away, Mrs. Grove would probably send him to fetch me. I could only stand and suffer.

Outside, a car engine started.

"Stop the caterer!" Mrs. Grove ordered Mike.

"Ma'am?"

Shoving him aside, she ran out the back door.

Mike looked at me. "Did I say something?" Then he sniffed. "I think you have a fire."

"We know," Sherman told him. "We're working on it."

Mike hesitated, then said to Sherman, Mona, and Lisa, "I'm Mike Harbinger."

Through the open kitchen window, I heard Sherman's mother discussing things with the caterer. He matched her shriek for shriek, then drove off.

"Was this a bad time to show up?" Mike asked me.

He stepped aside as Mrs. Grove marched in the back door. "A man who has no patience with dogs

109

and children should not be allowed to deal with the public." She looked around the room. "What has he been doing?" Stepping to the counter at the right of the sink, she ripped a few paper towels from a holder. She blotted the olive juice, then used the soaked towels to sweep the olives into the sink.

Mona snatched the colander of shrimp out of her way.

Shirley came through the swinging door. She was wearing a swirling gray dress with a low neckline. "I've got the fireplace under control. Is it safe to wash up in here?" Then she saw my hair. She stood for a second, transfixed.

"The caterer has abandoned us." Mrs. Grove did have a flair for making announcements rather than mere statements. "The guests will be arriving at any moment. The plumbing is still backed up, and I am thinking of leaving myself."

"You'd better put some shoes on and greet people." Shirley stepped over to the sink and turned on the faucets. "I'll help in here."

Mrs. Grove marched to the swinging door like Marie Antoinette to the guillotine, shoved it open, and stepped through.

I stood there, still holding Jake. It was not enough for fate to trap me at this party with a shorn head and Mike Harbinger. Impossible though it seemed, things had taken a turn for the worse. Now, I had to work in the same kitchen with a woman who had dumped my unsuspecting father for a rich slumlord.

110

Shirley finished rinsing her hands and turned to me. "Why are you holding that dog, Dez?" she asked. She didn't even seem uncomfortable talking to the daughter of the man she had betrayed.

"I forgot," Sherman said. "I'm supposed to feed him."

"Better get it done, then," Shirley advised him.

As Sherman climbed up on the counter again, Mona lifted the colander out of his way and stepped back. Shirley eased over to the right-hand counter and moved containers away from Sherman's feet.

Putting the colander in the sink once more, Mona resumed shrimp peeling.

Shirley surveyed the array of bottles and cans and tubs and jars on the counter. She turned to Mike. "Why don't you start bringing some platters over?"

Lisa stood before the stacks of bread and crackers looking like somebody waiting in line to pay a bill. "I'll start passing stuff over," Shirley told her. "You can start constructing hors d'oeuvres."

Lisa glanced at Mona, who went on peeling shrimp.

At the center island, Mike began stacking platters.

Shirley peered into a few of the tubs. "Dip. Okay. We'll need bowls for those."

Mike stacked bowls on the platters.

"Wowee! Truffles." Shirley picked up a tiny can. "Your dad must have the election in the bag, Sherman."

111

Sherman looked down at the can. "Truffles are a fungus, right?"

"Keep in mind that mushrooms are, too." Shirley stuck the can under the electric opener.

"Truffles grow underground and pigs dig them up," Sherman added.

"And people pay five hundred dollars a pound for them." Shirley opened a can of mushroom pâté and a jar of pimientos. "As a matter of fact, only a caterer can afford a can as big as the one I opened."

Mona looked at the truffles and then at Lisa. Lisa looked at the truffles, then at Mona. I wondered how many days' rent, theirs or ours, were in those few ounces of fungus.

Shirley went on opening cans and jars and bottles.

As Mike carried a stack of platters to Lisa, she cleared a place on the counter for them.

I was still holding Jake.

Sherman surveyed the top shelf. "Let's see. He had that yesterday. He's tired of that. That he won't eat." Finally he handed a can of dog food down to Shirley. "Would you open this for me?"

"Sure."

As she opened the can, Jake began struggling to get at it.

"Hey, come on." Mike sauntered over to me and stroked Jake's head. "You're a nice little guy," Mike told him.

Jake kissed his hand.

It was too much for me. Handing the dog to Mike, I stood back from all the action.

Mona lifted the colander to rinse off the shrimp.

"Snake!" Bramwell Grove shouted, as he came through the side door.

Bags and boxes fell out of the cupboard as Sherman grabbed a shelf. Shirley dropped the can of dog food and held his leg to steady him. Mona threw her hands in the air, along with the colander. Lisa yelled. I looked around for something we could coax a snake into.

"Hey! Hey! Keep it down! You're getting crazy in here," Bramwell admonished. "Sherman, check the garage for a snake."

Bracing her hands on the counter, Shirley closed her eyes for a moment. Then she spoke very carefully. "He means he wants a plumber's snake, Sherman. A plumber's snake is a long piece of metal for cleaning drains. You may find it coiled up, hanging on the wall in your garage. That is where a plumber's snake is kept in your average household."

Bramwell stared at my hair. "Oh." His *oh* was that of a man who has seen a grievous thing. He looked at Mona and Lisa, who were picking shrimp off the counters. "You let a little girl talk you into doing that? Don't you people have any sense of responsibility?"

I was too outraged to speak, even to defend Mona and Lisa. Here was the man basically responsible for my Varathaned hair, accusing the people who had tried to help me deal with it.

Shirley helped Sherman off the counter and fished cans and jars and bags and boxes out of the scatter of shrimp in the sink.

"Listen," Bramwell told Mona and Lisa. "You two run interference out there. One of you take the first floor, the other the upstairs. Head off anybody who tries to use a bathroom."

"Bramwell," Shirley protested.

"You want me to send one of the kids to do it?" With his jacket off and his sleeves up, Bramwell looked especially dashing, like some rich landowner who's been rounding up his horses before the tropical hurricane strikes. "The press will be here any minute. How would it look across the front page: Plumbing Erupts, Disrupts . . ."

"Never mind," Shirley said wearily.

"This has got to be it." Sherman staggered in, dragging a great coil of metal, thicker than my thumb and ten or twelve feet long. He lurched across the kitchen to his uncle, the snake scraping the floor.

Bramwell hoisted the snake to his own shoulder effortlessly. "Okay, ladies. Front and center."

Mona and Lisa followed Bramwell, leaving a floor littered with shrimp.

Recalling that I had actually mentioned the man's name in the beauty shop, I realized I'd been lucky to get off with nothing worse than the haircut I had.

114

"Do you have a laundry tub?" Shirley asked Sherman.

"Sure," he said.

"Why don't you scrub your hands out there, and then feed your dog—out there. I'd better go help with the plumbing."

She left, and Mike tried to calm Jake, who was struggling to get at the shrimp.

"How can she?" I exploded. "How *can* she?"

"Bram's an artist," Sherman said. "I've seen him collect rents. What he does is keep people off balance. One minute he's . . ."

"Unbearable," I said.

"He projects . . ."

"Obnoxiousness."

"Confidence," Sherman went on, "as if there's no question but that he's going to get what he wants, no matter who's in the way. The next minute, he's charming, so that nobody can keep up with his changes."

"Can't she *see*?" I demanded.

"Of course she sees," Sherman told me. "That's what makes him so interesting, if you're not doing business with him. A wolf is more intriguing than a dog."

"Thanks. Thanks a lot," I said.

"Come on, Dez. I didn't mean that."

Mike shifted his grip on Jake. "When are you going to feed this dog?"

"Let him eat shrimp," I snapped.

"That is rotten, really rotten." Sherman began

collecting shrimp off the floor. "Just because Shirley dumps your father, you take it out on my dog."

"I don't think one or two shrimp would hurt him," Mike ventured.

"He's not used to them." Sherman stood and threw a handful of shrimp into the sink. "They could upset his stomach."

They could, I realized, and I was instantly ashamed. You don't make smart cracks about anything that could hurt a dog.

Maneuvering Jake under one arm, Mike stroked him with his free hand. "That was very good, how you figured that character out," he told Sherman.

"Character?" Sherman knelt to pick up a few more shrimp.

"Your uncle. Bramwell. The slumlord," I told Sherman.

What am I saying? I thought. *How can I be so nasty?*

Sherman stood and dropped the shrimp in the sink. "That's okay," he told Mike. "Bramwell is a character."

It seemed the whole world was upside down this day. Now Sherman Grove was trying to put Mike Harbinger at ease.

"Listen," Mike assured Sherman, "relatives can be harder to figure out than strangers. You're good at it."

Sherman was overcome with confusion. Not only was somebody offering him respect, the somebody

116

was Mike Harbinger. "Well, I . . . I think about people a lot."

"He reads everything," I put in hastily, trying to redeem myself. *Born to Win; I'm O.K., You're O.K.; When I Say No, I Feel Guilty*—he's got them all upstairs."

"I've never read much psychology." Mike put Jake down. "I like books about science, though."

Jake scurried back and forth, sniffing the floor.

"Did you ever read *The Medusa and the Snail?*" Sherman asked Mike. "Or *The Crack in the Cosmic Egg* or *The Dragons of Eden?*"

"I've never even heard of them," Mike confessed.

"I could loan them to you," Sherman offered hesitantly.

"Great!" Mike said. "Should we feed the dog before he gets any more frustrated?"

Sherman took a can off the counter and headed for the back door with Mike. Jake followed.

"Do you have a computer?" Sherman asked Mike. The door closed behind them.

Left alone in the kitchen, I washed my hands. I let the cold water run as I shoved the shrimp and shells into the drain, then turned on the garbage disposal. To my relief, the shrimp and the water went down.

I knew that if we didn't get some food into the dining room, Mrs. Grove would soon be even more frantic. I transferred the rest of the bowls and trays and platters from the cooking island to the serving

117

cart, and wheeled it over to the counter at the left of the sink. Shrimp were scattered among the bread slices and cracker boxes.

The counter to the right of the sink was a jumble of tubs and jars and cans and bottles, stray shrimp, and the bags of chips and boxes of cereal that Sherman had knocked off the shelf.

It seemed wise to work with what I could identify. Clearing a space on the counter in front of me, I pulled the cart over and selected a few bowls and trays. Then I spooned what I was almost certain was guacamole dip from a tub into a bowl and put the bowl on a tray. After I arranged corn chips around the bowl, I began to feel encouraged. I filled another bowl with what looked as if it might be clam dip and surrounded it with potato chips.

Mike and Sherman came in from the garage, both talking at once. I arranged some barbecue chips around what was very likely a blue cheese dip.

"Hey, neat!" Sherman passed one tray to Mike and took another.

Holding the trays high like waiters, they carried my handiwork into the dining room.

Guests seemed to be arriving in droves. I could hear talking, even laughing, getting louder and louder. Though I was feeling a lot of pressure to get more food out there, I began to get caught up in the challenge. I brought bread and crackers over to the right-hand counter, and started spreading them with whatever was opened and seemed like the right consistency. Some of the stuff in the cans smelled pretty rank, but what did I know about gourmet food?

Mike and Sherman returned. "We're just putting everything on the dining room table," Sherman said.

"That's okay with me." I went on working.

Sherman began gathering up shrimp from the counter.

"There must be a hundred people out there," Mike told me, as if he talked to girls with stubble cuts every day.

"Pat Troup's here, too." Sherman put the shrimp on a platter.

When the people with you act as if you look fine, you begin to forget that you don't. "You mean as a reporter?" I asked.

"Naturally. My parents would only invite *editors* socially."

Mike shook pickled onions out of an open jar onto the platter.

"Wait a minute," I said to Sherman. "This party is for your dad to tell all these important people that he's running for mayor, before he announces it publicly."

Sherman emptied a jar of mixed nuts around the shrimp and onions. "There's no point inviting important people if it's not in the paper that they were here. It's an evening paper, Dez, and this is Sunday. The story of the party and the story of his announcement at the press conference will be in the same edition tomorrow."

Mike opened a box of little crackers and handed it to me. "It's very important to important people that everybody knows the candidate told them he was running before he told anybody else."

"Right." Sherman circled the nuts with a ring of marinated mushrooms. "There's more to politics, Dez, than anybody who's not in it suspects."

I kept on spreading one thing after another on bread and crackers. Mike and Sherman carried trays and platters into the dining room.

We were looking around for more serving dishes when Mrs. Grove came charging into the kitchen, carrying one of the platters I'd filled. "This will not do at all! At all!" She slammed the tray down before me on the center island. "You must garnish the canapés. And *who* is dumping cocktail onions and marinated mushrooms and nuts on the same tray? This is not a scout jamboree!"

She stormed back into the dining room.

Ordinarily, Sherman would have been upset by his mother's display, but being accepted by Mike Harbinger had made him a little reckless. "Garnish. Garnish." He ambled over to the counter and held up an unopened jar of pimientos. "This has got to be garnish. Nobody would eat it plain."

"We'd better get rid of some of this junk so we'll know the garnish from the garbage," Mike said.

"There are paper bags under the sink," Sherman told him.

120

Mike took a bag from under the sink, opened it, and put it on the floor. He began tossing empty containers from my counter into it.

Shirley came in from the dining room and went to the refrigerator. "Bring me a bowl, somebody. We need more ice for the bar."

I went on with my work. Sherman took her a bowl.

Bramwell stuck his head in. "Somebody has to drive Councilman Barrows to a service station," he told Shirley. "You want to come along?"

She handed the bowl to Sherman and left with Bramwell.

"She does seem to be getting flighty," Sherman told me.

Mike scooped up more empty cans from the counter.

"Hey!" Sherman grabbed his arm. "What did that label say?"

Mike put the cans down on the counter again. "Which one?"

"That one." Sherman's voice dwindled.

Mike picked up the can Sherman was staring at. "It's just dog food . . ."

Sherman dashed toward the laundry room, Mike and me behind him.

seven

Jake's dish was on the floor. Sherman reached into the wastebasket beside the dryer and drew out a lint-covered can, which he held as if it were a scorpion. He blew the lint off the can, but then his courage failed him, and he handed the can to Mike, who looked at it soberly.

"Um . . . your dog just ate a fortune in truffles," Mike told him gently.

Sherman groaned. "Just changing dog food *brands* upsets his stomach."

"Wait. Wait." Dreadful as it was, someone had to say it. "If you fed Jake the can of truffles, and the dog food can in the kitchen is empty—"

We raced back through the kitchen, Jake with us. As Mike shoved open the swinging door, Jake shot past him into the dining room.

There must have been more than a hundred people standing with their backs to us. Before us was the long dining room table, with a huge ice sculpture in the shape of our City Hall and flowers and linens and silver and china—and plates and plates of the canapés I'd made so efficiently, the canapés Sherman and Mike had carried so cheerfully through the swinging doors.

The guests were gathered at the other end of the dining room, where it joined the living room.

Most of them were holding drinks and little plates of food. Everyone was quiet as Harley Grove spoke. Even the dog was silent as he strolled into the crowd.

"Sherman," I whispered, "I can't tell which canapés have what on them."

Mike reached for a platter. "Let's get them all off the table."

"But what about the ones the people already took?" I tried to keep my voice steady.

I couldn't see Harley Grove over the crowd, but he certainly didn't sound like a man who'd been struggling with fires and plumbing. Of course, he didn't know about the refreshments yet.

His voice was deep and rich and sincere. "And I promise you all an administration dedicated to reform, to progress, to prosperity . . ."

I heard Sherman take a quick deep breath before he yelled, "DON'T ANYBODY SWALLOW ANYTHING!"

The crowd parted as Mrs. Grove advanced upon us like a storm trooper. She shoved Sherman through the swinging door so fast that Mike and I had to back into the kitchen or be flattened by him.

"How dare you!" Mrs. Grove gave Sherman another shove.

123

A silver-haired man charged in from the dining room. Behind him came Mrs. Harbinger and then Pat Troup, carrying Jake.

"Sherman tried to help!" Mike Harbinger told Mrs. Grove.

The silver-haired man grabbed Mike's arm. "You keep out of this!"

"Dad, will you just be calm?" Mike sounded aggrieved but patient.

"You take your hands off him!" Mike's mother flared at his father.

"Hey! Hey! Hey!" Bramwell came through the swinging door, Shirley behind him. "What are you landing all over the kids for?"

Mrs. Grove suddenly noticed Pat Troup. "Do you mind?" she snapped.

"Whose dog?" Pat asked me. "He doesn't seem to like councilmen."

"Mom," Sherman said desperately, "we've got to get the canapés away from the people out there."

"Don't try to change the subject!"

Looking at me, Mike jerked his head toward the dining room. As I eased toward the door, Mrs. Grove straightened. "Don't you dare set a foot in there, Desdemona Blank!"

Sherman looked ready to cry. "Mom, what they've got in there are dog-food canapés."

His mother's hands slid down his arms. She sank into a squat, her elbows on her knees and her head in her hands. "Don't explain. Don't."

"Dear?" Opening the swinging door, Mr. Grove

looked in. His face was drawn, but his voice was bright and hearty. "The last guests are leaving, dear. Won't you come out and say goodbye?"

Bramwell helped Mrs. Grove up. She tried to head for the back door, but he turned her toward the dining room, and the Harbingers followed her through. They must have been good friends of hers, or very staunch supporters of Harley's.

"Dog-food canapés?" Shirley asked Sherman.

"I got the cans mixed up, so I dumped truffles in the dog dish and we spread dog food on the bread and crackers."

We. Even in despair, Sherman was careful to protect me.

"You print a word about this..." Bramwell warned Pat.

"I wouldn't wait until tomorrow's edition to tell your guests they ate dog food," she said.

"Oh, come on," Bramwell scoffed. "Nobody's going to eat canned dog food. Did you ever *smell* the stuff? I wouldn't feed it to my dog."

"Dog? You mean Jake?" Harley Grove reentered the kitchen with his wife and the Harbingers. "The dog who attacked Councilman Barrows? The dog who belongs to my son? My son, who is dedicated to the destruction of my political future, my social life, any position I had in this community, not to mention my mental health."

"Come off it, Harley," Mrs. Harbinger said. "You're going to scar your child for life."

Glancing at Pat Troup, Mrs. Grove patted her

husband's arm. "Harley. Harley, it will all look brighter tomorrow."

He glared at Pat. "It will all look much darker tomorrow, in bold black print."

"I'm a reporter, not a gossip columnist," she said coldly.

"I respect that," Bramwell declared. "And the dog food was approved by the Department of Agriculture. Nobody will get sick from eating dog-food canapés. On the other hand, it would probably make them sick to read that they ate them."

"Dog-food canapés?" Harley Grove looked at his brother wildly.

Mrs. Grove put a firm hand on Bramwell's arm. "It's been a long day, and I know you all want to help us clean up, but we can take care of it. We don't want to keep you lovely people. The party is over—all's well that ends well."

"Ends well? More than a hundred guests inhaling soot. Guests who approach the bathroom and are harassed by two women in pink uniforms and great monuments of technologically advanced hair . . ." Harley Grove drew a deep breath as Mona and Lisa strolled in from the hall.

Mrs. Grove never stopped smiling, but she kept her grip on her husband's arm.

He seemed to have a need to talk. "We spend a fortune for a caterer, and the food comes out looking like party snacks for a fraternity hazing. When I finally announce my candidacy, my son, my own flesh and blood, bursts in, bellowing, *'Don't swallow anything!'* " Mr. Grove pried his wife's fingers off his arm. "I had every reason to expect this day to end in congratulations, pledges, donations. Instead, more than one hundred people skulked out of here like the survivors of a weekend at the Draculas'.... Dog-food canapés?"

"Later, dear," Mrs. Grove told him.

Everyone else was silent. Everyone seemed drained.

Everyone but Mona and Lisa. They leaned against the refrigerator, looking more relaxed than I'd ever seen them.

Mrs. Harbinger took the caterer's apron off the food processor. "There's nothing to do about it now, except clean up."

She was right. I'd come there with fantasies of winning over Sherman's parents and uncle. Instead, I had helped create a calamity they'd never forget. I suspected that if Pat Troup hadn't been there, they'd have ordered me out long ago.

"I'll just take out some of the trash." Bramwell picked up a bag. "Then we've got to get going. My dog will be thinking I'm never coming back."

"You want a ride?" Pat asked me.

I hesitated. "My father . . ." I glanced at Shirley, but she was busy throwing canapés into the sink.

"Why don't you call him?" Pat suggested. "Tell him I'll run you home."

After tormenting you mercilessly, fate tosses you

a token favor. At least I didn't have to worry about arranging my departure so that my father wouldn't run into Shirley.

He was home, of course, and happy to hear that he didn't have to come out again.

I got my coat and tied on Mrs. Farisee's scarf, although it didn't matter anymore.

Pat was in the foyer wearing a plum-color tweed cape and her loose-knit green-and-tan-and-purple Dr. Who muffler. She glanced into the parlor, where Mona and Lisa were collecting empty glasses. "Anybody need a ride?"

"Thanks anyway," Mona said. "We told Mr. Wonderful we'd stick around until he's ready to leave."

"Besides," Lisa added, "we want to see how it turns out."

Mona watched Pat toss the muffler around her head and shoulders. "Who does your hair?" she asked.

"In the annals of weird," Pat observed, as her car wheezed and sputtered into life, "that party will live forever. You're not going to cry, are you?"

"Not if I can help it." The next thing I knew, I was telling her about my polyurethaned hair and the Groves' condominium plans.

"I thought that if I helped them in an emergency, they might be so grateful they'd at least find us another place to live if they did sell our house. And you saw what happened."

"Condos," Pat said. "They're a plague. Instead of fixing up perfectly livable little houses, the owners sell them to developers who tear them down and put up fancy buildings the people they evicted can't afford to live in. There was a rash of them years ago, and the builders lost their shirts. But the craze is starting again. I'm going to write a series on it."

"Will that do any good?"

"Probably not. The City Council is all for redevelopment and the big moneylenders have a stake in it."

"You're going to write about it anyway?"

"That's my job. I guess a reporter always thinks that if she can explain what's going on, it may make a difference. That's supposed to compensate for our lousy wages."

She drove on for another block. I was quiet, thinking how I was obsessed with my haircut, which was nothing compared to a family and three dogs without a home.

"This deal," Pat said, "has some interesting ingredients. We've got Harley, running for mayor, pushing through the condo conversions, and presently owning the houses that will be razed for them. We've got his brother, who you say will be buying the houses. Then we've got my dad, refusing to make it easy for them. When he hears that they're planning to destroy his house for a condo. . . ." She grinned. "He wouldn't sell now for anything."

I couldn't see what she was so optimistic about. "Can't they make him? Sherman said that since

129

Bramwell will own most of the houses on the block, it should be a cinch to get your father's condemned."

"Ah ha! But now we come to the crucial ingredients, the wild cards. We've got Desdemona Blank, and Pat Troup, ace reporter. They were at the party at which over one hundred backers of Harley Grove's mayoral campaign were served dog food. Both you and I know we would never lower ourselves to hold that over the Groves. But *they* don't. Neither your father nor mine is in any danger of being forced to find another dwelling for a long, long time."

I just rode along for a while, letting it sink in that we might actually be safe. Within a few blocks, I could even think about other people's problems. "I hope Sherman's parents won't be too rough on him."

"He's kind of a wispy kid."

"Most people think he's a wimp." Then I told her what my father had said about wimps.

Her face grew stern and her voice was firm. "No. Not Bruce Springsteen. Never. Bruce Springsteen is reason to believe."

I hoped she wasn't going to start talking religion, but I had to ask. "In what?"

"The species."

When we stopped at my house, she said, "Listen, your hair will grow. Look at me. I won't."

"Lots of guys like short girls."

"Big deal. You know how far that gets you in my line of work? Half my life, I've been fighting *cute.*"

When I came in, my father turned off "60 Minutes." He was still in his suit trousers and shirt, and he hadn't even taken off his shoes. I suppose he wanted to be ready to hurry out if Shirley called.

I could hear the television in the bedroom and the radio in Mrs. Farisee's room.

I couldn't help thinking of the Groves, three people in a house so big they couldn't even hear one another most of the time: three people with three and a half bathrooms.

On the other hand, ours was working.

"How was it?" My father tossed the TV listing on an end table, to make room for me beside him on the sofa.

I took off my coat and the scarf and sat down. "You don't want to know."

I told him anyway, the whole dreadful business.

"... So I wrecked the party by making dog-food canapés—which are probably all that will keep him from kicking us out of this house. Pat says they'll think we might use the canapés against them."

"Sure they will, because they'd use it if the positions were reversed. So you saved your family and our dogs—not to mention Mr. Troup."

"Mr. Troup wouldn't thank me if I saved this whole town."

Putting an arm around me, my father pulled me closer. "He might find it hard to say 'Thank you,

Desdemona, for serving dog food to your landlord's guests.' That's true. But remember that your intentions were noble, and the outcome will be fine."

That did it. "You know, if anybody had tried to tell me an hour ago that I would ever smile again, I would have been insulted."

He cuddled my head against his shoulder and ran a hand over my hair. "Feels like a Chesapeake Bay retriever." Then he got serious. "Harley can't lose this election, Dez. He's got the paper and most of the City Council behind him—even Councilman Barrows, public rest room or no." He was quiet for a minute, and I could tell he wasn't thinking of me or of elections. "You say Shirley was there with Harley's brother?"

I sat up so I could look at him. "I wasn't sure I should tell you, but I decided it would be better if I did. You won't have to try to look unsurprised if you hear about it from somebody else."

He nodded. "You were right."

"I thought you and she were getting along."

"So did I."

"You feel bad?"

"Yes."

I noticed that he'd been biting his cuticles again. He probably did it rather than smoke, which might leave his children prematurely fatherless. He was a good man, kind to children and dogs, and I couldn't understand why things seemed to go right for him so seldom. "There's got to be something wrong with her."

"Of course," he said gravely. "Who's going to take a rich, handsome bachelor with a thirty-thousand-dollar car over a married father of three who's renting a two-bedroom house from . . ."

I pulled away. "That really bothers me, when you make jokes to cover up how you feel. I'm serious. What does she see in him?"

"Aside from . . ."

"No, come on. Don't. He's . . ."

"Crass? Abrasive?"

"At his best. And all you know about him is what I've told you, remember?"

"What about the dog? What about him defending you and Sherman at the party?"

"Mrs. Harbinger defended Mike and Sherman, but that doesn't make her Mother of the Year. You're not going to tell me Bramwell has a heart of gold."

"I'm saying there's probably a lot more to him than you see. Look how different from Harley he is. Did they grow up as privileged as you'd guess from meeting Harley, or on the mean streets you'd expect from what you saw of Bramwell? Maybe what fascinates Shirley is that he is so complex."

My father was actually getting absorbed in his analysis. The man had just been *dumped,* and he was getting into character studies. For a second, I could see how he could drive a woman dating him right to somebody who reacted more and talked less. Immediately, I felt disloyal. "But Shirley's so different from Sherman's uncle," I protested.

"She's not engaged to him, Dez. Besides, do you think I'm attracted only to women with high I.Q.'s and higher principles?"

I did not smile. I laughed, just thinking of the women he had dated after my mother left and before he met Shirley. "They run together in my mind—a lot of lip gloss and satin blouses and barely voting age."

The telephone rang and he went to answer it.

He came back looking bemused. "Pat Troup. She wants to know if I'd like to go out for pizza."

I was amazed. "You going?"

"Sure."

"Oh, good." Pat was loaded with I.Q. and principles. Also, she was a woman of action, which is what a man who tends not to be needs.

After my father left, I went back to the bedroom. Preston and my brother were playing Chinese checkers on the floor while Preston talked, and talked. Neither of them greeted me.

When I left the room, Aida followed.

"Can't you tell them you want to play, too?" I asked her.

She shook her head and followed me to the parlor and didn't even object to the television program I selected.

After a while, a car's horn sounded.

A minute later, I heard someone knock on Mrs. Farisee's door, and then Preston's voice. "Good night, Mrs. Farisee. Thank you for the very nice time."

She walked him to the door, and helped him turn up the collar of his navy blue double-breasted wool coat.

"What a charmer," she said when he left. She looked at me. "How was the party?"

I turned down the set. "I think I'm getting the flu."

"You're going to school tomorrow. Your hair won't be that much longer Tuesday."

eight

I did feel sick when I woke and remembered my hair.

I knew it would do no good to appeal to my father. He'd tell me the same thing Mrs. Farisee had.

With five people and one bathroom, mornings are difficult, so we never chat at breakfast the way families are supposed to.

Aida seemed to have no more appetite than I, but both my father and Antony ate their waffles with zest.

When the telephone rang, Mrs. Farisee answered it, and then told the caller, "After this, don't phone at breakfast time."

That gave me no clue who it was. Mrs. Farisee wouldn't hesitate to instruct the President not to call us at breakfast time.

"For you," she told Antony.

"May I be excused?" Aida asked, when he went to the telephone.

"Isn't anybody going to eat this morning?" my father demanded.

Aida left the table.

My brother came back. "Can I go to Preston's after school?" he asked my father.

"*May* I go, and did his mother invite you?"

Antony nodded. "She'll drive me home."

"Fine. But hurry up and finish your breakfast." My father poured himself another cup of coffee.

Sherman arrived to walk to school with Antony and me.

Walking to school with Mrs. Farisee's paisley print scarf on, I was grateful for the company of even my brother and an eleven-year-old kid.

"How's Jake?" I asked Sherman.

"Fine. Kind of put out that he didn't get truffles for breakfast."

"What happened after I left?"

"My father stewed and my mother went to bed with a migraine right after the Harbingers left."

Neither of us mentioned Bramwell buying our house. Sherman probably didn't want to remind me of how seriously I'd offended his parents. I certainly wasn't going to bring up the reason we'd probably be staying. You don't tell your best friend that his parents would think you capable of blackmail.

Ahead of us, I saw some people walking to school. Suddenly, a roof over my head meant nothing compared to the stubble on my head. "Sherman, I'm going to be sick. I'm going to be sick right here on

137

the sidewalk. This scarf is bad enough, but I can never, never show my hair to a whole school."

He stopped. "You don't want anybody to notice you, so you're going to throw up. You want humiliation, try throwing up in public. I did, my first day in kindergarten. Right in the classroom."

He walked on, and I fell into step, rather than be left with only a five-year-old.

"I'm talking instant celebrity," Sherman continued somberly. "Everybody yells and jumps away and makes a big production of pretending to gag. Then the custodian comes along with a ton of sawdust and cleans up, and all day everybody goes 'Yuck' when you come near."

My brother walked between us, gazing up at Sherman with awe.

I was impressed, in spite of myself. "How about if I just pass out?"

He didn't even look at me. "Great way to be inconspicuous. With any luck, somebody will call an ambulance, and they'll roar up with that old red light flashing and load you on a stretcher and rush you to the emergency room and call your father at work . . ."

"Sherman, I am truly, physically sick." I was not exaggerating. My heart seemed to be moving up in my chest, crowding my lungs, squeezing all the breath out of me.

We had reached the corner of the street Mike Harbinger usually came down. Since I didn't dare turn back and go home, the only thing to do now was hurry on. I walked faster, looking straight ahead.

"Hey, Sherman!"

I knew the voice.

Mike Harbinger was hailing Sherman Grove.

I was so astonished, I looked before I thought.

"Hey, Antony!" Preston broke away from the group trailing his brother and ran toward us.

Sherman stopped. Antony stopped.

When Mike Harbinger yelled, everybody looked. It was too late to run.

Preston started talking even before he reached us. Behind him came a gaggle of boys about my brother's size. Closing rapidly were Mike and his friends.

I don't know whether my legs simply failed me, or whether my reactions to the stresses of the last few days reached a critical point. Suddenly I was sitting on somebody's front lawn.

"Hey." Dropping his books beside me, Mike hunkered down to peer in my face. "Are you all right, Dez?"

I should have thrown up when I had the chance, I thought. *I should have fainted.* A person like me could do almost anything without attracting the notice she'd get just by being with Mike Harbinger.

"You look pale." His face was only inches from mine. "You want me to walk you home?"

"She's all right," Sherman said. "She just doesn't want to show her hair."

I could sink my teeth into his ankle, I thought,

139

but he probably has his tetanus boosters up to date.

"What's the matter with your hair?" Mike asked me.

"You ought to see it," Preston told the little kids around him. "Like she ran her head through a lawn mower."

Mike sat down beside me. "We'll wait for a few minutes. Then if you don't feel better I'll phone somebody to come get you. Preston, you guys go on."

"Go ahead," I told my brother.

As Antony walked away with Preston and Preston's group, Mike yelled after them, "Hey! You two come directly home after school, hear?"

Preston nodded and waved and kept talking to Antony.

Mike looked up at Sherman, who stood over us. "I tried the computer program you showed me after the party, but I'm still missing something."

Sherman sat down to explain. Mike's friends sat down to listen. Every few words, one of them would interrupt with a question—for Sherman.

"I still don't get it," Mike said finally.

"Why don't we all go to my house after school and you can show us." A tall dark-haired boy with a tan that made him look like a ski instructor had been frowning over Sherman's explanation. "I've got a hard disk and dual drives," he told Sherman, as if presenting his credentials.

"He's also got an eight-millimeter camcorder and

a laser disk player with Dolby hi-fi remote stereo," a redhead added.

"And every video Huey Lewis ever made," the dark-haired boy said modestly.

"You're kidding!" Sherman gasped.

"Right back to 'Do You Believe in Love?' and 'Workin' for a Livin'.' Maybe you can figure out why I'm still getting noise on my tapes."

We sat there, Sherman and I, surrounded by high school superstars talking about their computers and audio and video equipment.

Mike looked at me. "Are you going to be all right?" he asked.

I nodded.

He gathered up my books and even steadied me as I stood. Then he and his friends walked Sherman and me to the junior high school, Mike carrying my books. I would have felt stupid letting him, except that I knew he was doing it because I was feeling shaky, not because I was a female.

As we approached the school's entrance, crowds parted before us.

I realized, suddenly and very clearly, that I could get away with my haircut. I could get away with having Sherman for a friend. I could get away with anything short of double-knit polyester.

Mike Harbinger had walked to school with me.

"I'm okay now." I took my books. "Thanks."

"Meet you here at three-thirty," he told Sherman.

"You can call home from my house," said the boy

with the Dolby hi-fi remote stereo video disk player.

Sherman watched them walk on toward the high school. "Can you imagine my parents if I went any-place but your house without calling for permission *first*?"

All around us, people were watching us, so he kept his voice low. "I'm going to have to go to the office and try to con the school secretary into letting me use the phone."

I thought of Sherman calling from school for permission to hang out with a bunch of high school luminaries, and I struggled to keep my face solemn.

"It's not funny." He looked hurt.

I walked in the front door with him. "I'm just picturing all those overprivileged overachievers in their classy watches and sixty-dollar shirts sitting around listening to 'Workin' for a Livin'."

"Hey, twenty years from now those Huey Lewis tapes will still be classics."

"I know! I know! Would Mike Harbinger's associ-ates be guilty of having less-than-impeccable taste? And twenty years from now . . . No. No, they won't be selling cars or working in little offices. They'll own their family's dealerships and law firms, but they'll still be telling everybody how they used to watch those old music videos with you."

"You're crazy this morning, you know that?"

"Sure I'm crazy. Suddenly, I don't see you as eleven. You're almost twelve. Mike Harbinger talks to you."

"You don't have to be so sarcastic about him. He likes you."

I grabbed Sherman's sleeve, right there in the crowded hall. "How do you know?"

"After you left yesterday, he said you were neat. He asked how old you were."

It was too much. I let my hand drop.

"I told him thirteen."

"Sherman." Naturally, I couldn't embarrass my best friend by saying *I love you.*

"He also likes your hair," Sherman added.

I dodged in front of him. *"What? What?"*

"He says it reminds him of Annie."

"Annie?"

"Annie Lennox. You know, the Eurythmics singer."

"You let me suffer all morning and you didn't tell me?"

"I forgot."

I would have chased him to his locker, but I wasn't so secure that I would deliberately make a scene while wearing a paisley print scarf on my head.

As I turned down the corridor to my own locker, two girls fell into step with me.

"How long have you known him?" Marti Dunnigan was our class president. Her best friend, Kerri White, had nominated her, and then Marti nominated Kerri for vice-president, and they both won.

"Sherman?" I asked.

"Him." Kerri's voice was urgent. "You know."

"Oh, Mike. We went to the van Gogh exhibit Saturday night, and we were at a party yesterday."

Marti smote her own forehead with the heel of her hand. "Art? He likes *art*? And I went *skating* Saturday!"

Kerri, who had never worn the same sweater twice in a month, picked a piece of lint off my sleeve.

I hung my coat in my locker and fussed around with my books.

"You forgot to take your scarf off," Kerri reminded me.

I didn't feel like the girl Mike had walked to school with, suddenly.

I could make a dash for the rest room, but I couldn't cower in there all day. I could say I was sick, but Mrs. Farisee wouldn't let me stay home. If I went anywhere else, the school would call my house, and then I'd be in trouble that would make my hours at the Groves' party seem pleasant.

There was no way out. Someday, I knew, I would look back on this moment, and it would still seem excruciating.

I took off the scarf.

Marti struck her forehead again. "How did you make your folks *let* you?"

I was still the girl who had walked to school with Mike Harbinger. Everything about me was right. Especially my hair, because nobody in the school had a cut like mine, and Mike Harbinger had walked to school with me.

144

"My mother would kill me if I even showed her a picture of a cut like that!" Kerri stared at me. "I had to beg for months just to get tinted contact lenses! How did you talk your folks into it?"

"I didn't."

She was staggered. "You mean you just went down and got it cut?"

It's hard work to maintain a pose. "Actually," I confessed, "it got Varathaned, and—"

"You mean like *varnished*?" Marti cried, with such feeling that a couple of other girls hurried over to us.

"She varnished her hair!" Kerri announced.

Teena Brannigan edged past Kerri to touch my hair. "It *is*! It's stiff!"

"Let me see." Laurelle Carson patted my head.

Marti stepped back to squint at me. "You know what would be fan*tas*tic? If you colored it, maybe platinum, or red."

Kerri cast her a look of cold disdain. "That would look like she was *trying*."

"Does Mike like it?" Teena asked.

I wondered if there was anybody in the school building who hadn't seen me with him, or heard about it already.

"Of course he likes it," Kerri said. "He walked to school with her, didn't he?"

"So who did you get to cut it for you without your parents' permission?" Kerri pressed.

"The Mona Lisa," I said, "but only because it was a special case."

145

I started for my homeroom. To be one of the last few sauntering in would be just like challenging my teacher. Laurelle, Teena, Marti, and Kerri fell into step with me, along with three girls who usually cut ahead of me whenever I bought my lunch.

Marti walked backward so she could face me. "The Mona Lisa?"

"In the Rancho Grande Mall," I said.

"That old place? I never knew they could do hair like that!"

Teena looked at her scornfully. "You think *I. Magnin* is going to cut hair like that?" She edged around Laurelle to walk next to me. "Would I have to take in a note from my mother?"

"Absolutely," I assured her. "Or take your mother."

Jerking her head toward me, Kerri told the line-crashers, "She went out with Mike Harbinger last Saturday and Sunday both."

"It wasn't like a date or anything." I think I was reassuring myself, more than anything else. "My father would never let me go out on a real date yet."

Cheryl reclaimed her position next to me. "My mother says I can't go out with boys until I'm *fifteen*."

I slowed down. "You know, there's a lot of stress involved in going anywhere with a guy, even when it's not a real date."

They were all quiet, walking slower, everybody with her own thoughts.

"Yeah," Kerri said finally. "You don't think

about that aspect—until you start thinking about it."

"So you're just kind of friends with Mike?" Marti asked.

I nodded. "We've been through a lot together."

"Imagine." Teena was solemn. "Mike Harbinger for your *friend*."

"But you like him, don't you?" one of the line-crashers prompted.

I stopped. "I do. I really do." I didn't truly realize it until I said it. "He's a nice guy."

Laurelle fell backward into Kerri's arms. "*A nice guy,*" she moaned.

At roll call, my homeroom teacher glanced at my hair and closed his eyes.

When I walked into my math class, the teacher told me I was wanted in the office. As I walked out, even boys threw me sympathetic grimaces and thumbs-up signs.

"Don't sit down," the school secretary greeted me. "Go right into the office before you attract more fans."

Ms. Cohen, our principal, looked at me across her desk. "I heard, but I still wasn't prepared. The rumor is that it's varnished, too."

I nodded.

Before I could speak, she went on. "I deplore mindless conformity. I respect individuality. It is nobody's business how you wear your hair, so long as it does not constitute a public health hazard. I'm just asking you, one human being to another,

147

whether this is the first shot in a campaign of organized rebellion."

I explained how I came to be Varathaned and shorn.

"I have to admit I'm relieved," she said when I'd finished.

"It could catch on," I warned.

"I can live with it. When I started college, and all the sorority types wore skirts and sweaters, my friends and I walked around barefoot carrying acoustic guitars and wearing bedspreads."

"Bedspreads?"

"Indian, from Cost Plus or Pier One. You fold it over, cut a hole for the head, sew up the sides from about the knees to the armpits..." She stopped suddenly. "Go back to class."

As I started for the door, she said, "I remember, when I was fifteen, my mother asked me why my generation had this irresistible urge to rile hers."

"What did you tell her?"

"I said, 'Because you're there.'"

"I don't want to rile anybody."

"You haven't hit your teens."

Being called to the office only magnified my renown. Everybody wanted to know what Ms. Cohen had said. I didn't mention the bare feet and bedspreads. She'd trusted me.

There's a proverb or something that says, "Be careful what you wish for. You might get it."

At lunch, so many people dragged chairs over to my table, I had to eat with my elbows wedged against my sides. I couldn't even see where Sherman was.

I had notes passed to me in all my classes.

So many people stopped me to talk after school that it was quarter to four by the time I got out of the building.

That part was okay. I wouldn't have wanted to be around when Mike and his friends came for Sherman. With all the twelve- and thirteen-year-old girls trailing me, there would have been just too much going on.

Of course, I doubted that fifteen-year-old males talking electronics would notice any junior high school girls.

What surprised me was that I missed Sherman.

I worried about him a little, too. There's a big gap between fifteen and even a brilliant twelve. By the time Mike and his friends got their driver's licenses, they'd be moving into a world where he'd be lost even as a mascot.

Marti and Kerri ran with me to my sister's school.

Aida was waiting on the sidewalk with a small, dark-haired girl and a slender, anxious-looking woman of about thirty.

Aida, who had scuffed out the right knee of her new jeans and spilled something down the front of her coat, started talking when I was yards away. "Here's my sister." She clutched the hand of the little girl, who smiled at me as if I were a friend from way back.

"This is Tran," Aida told me as I came closer. "She's in my class, and this is her mom. Before I left for school, I asked Mrs. Farisee if I could bring a friend home. It's okay with her, but I don't think it is with Mrs. Luan."

Mrs. Luan smiled at me, but she looked uncertain and embarrassed. She was not much taller than I. Like Tran, she had thick, lustrous, straight black hair and gorgeous almond-shaped eyes. Mrs. Luan wore a thin tan coat with cotton slacks and canvas sneakers. It was clear that what clothing money there was went to dress Tran.

Aida was hanging on to Tran's hand and looking at me as if I could fix everything.

I wasn't sure I could make myself understood, but it was cold and they must have been standing there waiting for me a long time. "See you guys later," I told Marti and Kerri.

They left, and I turned my attention to Mrs. Luan. "We are happy to have Tran come visit. We can even bring her home later, if you like."

Mrs. Luan listened politely, but she still seemed undecided.

I wasn't sure whether she had understood me, but I understood her look. It would be terrifying to just turn your kid loose in a strange country.

"Would you come, too?" I asked her. "Come to tea, please. Mrs. Farisee would want me to invite you." I wasn't sure about that last part, but we couldn't stand in the street negotiating forever.

"Today?" Mrs. Luan asked.

"Yes," I said. "Yes. Now."

"Oh." She smiled again, and she suddenly looked much younger. "Thank you. Yes. Thank you."

Aida and Tran bounded ahead and around and behind us like grasshoppers in spring.

Mrs. Luan's English was new and careful, but, block by block, she became more comfortable trying it out. By the time we got to my house, she'd told me that Tran was her only child, that they had been in this country six months, and that she found it very big and very cold.

You don't often bring a kid home from school with her mother, but Mrs. Farisee didn't betray her surprise. Since I had invited Mrs. Luan, I offered to make her tea. "Fine," Mrs. Farisee said. "I made chocolate chip cookies. They're on top of the fridge."

I was astonished. Aida's bringing home a friend must have been a great occasion in Mrs. Farisee's eyes, too.

I took Mrs. Luan's coat and left her in the parlor with Mrs. Farisee. I could hear them talking while I put on the kettle and set a tea tray.

Aida took Tran directly out to the backyard to meet Herb and Joe and Sadie. Hearing the riotous greetings, I hoped Mrs. Luan would think it was some other dogs in the neighborhood.

Fortunately, we had three good china cups without chipped rims.

Being well-adjusted dogs, ours settled down after the first thrill of meeting a new person. I could hear

151

Aida showing Tran around. "So this pile of rocks and wood will be our castle, and we and the dogs are the French soldiers in it. Monty Python and Sir Lance-a-Lot are attacking us, and we throw down horrible stuff and yell insults like—"

I ran to the back door. "Aida Blank!" I shouted.

When I carried the tray into the parlor, Mrs. Luan and Mrs. Farisee were chatting almost like neighbors.

After a cup of tea, I excused myself and called Aida and Tran in for cookies. Then I took some back to the bedroom.

It wasn't often I had our room to myself. I lay on my bed, reveling in the solitude. It wasn't much of a room, but at the moment it was all mine.

Of course, if anything developed between Pat Troup and my father, their combined salaries might qualify them for a mortgage.

Four bedrooms would be ideal, but we could scrape by with three, so long as we had two bathrooms.

I wondered how Pat would get along with Mrs. Farisee. She'd have to. We couldn't lose Mrs. Farisee.

One pizza, and I was casting Pat Troup as a potential stepmother. Ridiculous, maybe, but a healthy sign—as much as you may want somebody who's left you, you can't sit around waiting forever.

I felt more guilty about taking Mrs. Farisee for granted. Then I wondered about my assumption that any woman would rather be a reporter than a housekeeper. It might well be that Mrs. Farisee was doing the work she preferred. I wondered what she had wanted, or expected, or hoped for when she was young. I'd never ask her, of course, but it would be interesting if she took a notion to talk about it sometime.

We're separate countries, all of us, separate and mysterious, haunted by the times and places and people we've lost, or never had.

I could hear the women talking in the parlor, and Tran laughing with my sister outside.

There is reason to believe in the species, if you take us one by one.

I brought the dogs into my room. After dinner, I'd call old Sherman and see how he was doing.